PROJECT GEMINI
1998

An experimental, multi-leveled, secret scientific research community, hundreds of feet below a remote Texas town.

DR. BENJAMIN RICEMAN

A brilliant mind imprisoned in a frail body. His daydreams would become inescapable nightmares.

DR. MICHELLE MONTIGNAC

The last woman left in a man's world. She must face unknown terror . . . alone.

COLONEL C. P. SAXON

Part man, part machine. He possesses a secret that could destroy the universe.

GEMINI RISING

GEMINI RISING

J.S. FILBRUN

FAWCETT GOLD MEDAL • NEW YORK

To my wife Michelle. Without her constant encouragement, critical candor, and sharp stick, this work would never have been completed.

ARMAGEDDON

REVELATION 19:17-19

AND I SAW AN ANGEL STANDING
IN THE SUN; AND HE CRIED WITH A
LOUD VOICE, SAYING TO ALL THE FOWLS
THAT FLY IN THE MIDST OF HEAVEN,

"COME AND GATHER YOURSELVES TOGETHER
UNTO THE SUPPER OF THE GREAT GOD,
THAT YE MAY EAT THE FLESH OF KINGS,
AND THE FLESH OF CAPTAINS, AND THE
FLESH OF MIGHTY MEN, AND THE FLESH
OF HORSES, AND OF THEM THAT SIT ON
THEM, AND THE FLESH OF ALL MEN. . . ."

AND I SAW THE BEAST. . . .

HOLY BIBLE
KING JAMES VERSION

PROJECT GEMINI

LOCATION:

> 173 miles South South-East of El Paso, Texas
> Presidio County
> Smoke Tree Basin

COMPOUND:

> 731 yards wide
> 1627 yards long
> Enclosed by 12-foot electrified fence
> Guard towers: 8
> Helicopter pads: 2
> Support facilities for 500 personnel
> Misc:
>> Ammunition Bunker–Northeast Section (D)
>> Surplus Area–Northeast Section (D)
>> Storage Area–Northeast Section (D)

UNDERGROUND STRUCTURE:

> Diameter — 632 feet
> Depth — Main Structure–1200 feet
> — Main & Binary Bomb–1240 feet
> Support facilities for 400 personnel

UNDERGROUND STRUCTURE

Level One Depth: 1050′	Personnel Quarters; Executive Offices Security Command; Bruce Central Communications
Level Two Depth: 1082′	Cafeteria; Maintenance Medical Center; Personnel Quarters Recreation Center
Level Three Depth: 1124′	Research Center; Cyclotron Laser Facility
Level Four Depth: 1196′	Security Control Reconstruction Unknown

```
TIME      :  2238  11 JANUARY 1998
AREA      :  SECURITY CONTROL
LEVEL     :  4
SENSORS   :  6883–85
```

"NOT THIS TIME, YOU LITTLE RED BASTARD!" CORPORAL Jackson shouted at the small flashing light. His voice echoed around the compact room as he pounded his fists against the security console.

"You can beat your pukin' heart out, but ol' Jackson ain't gonna fall for that shit!" There was a note of uneasiness in his voice as he tried to convince himself. "If those dumb muthafuckers can't find what's wrong with you, I'm sure as hell not gonna lay my ass on the line again!"

With that, Jackson flopped down in his chair, swiveled away from the console, and began an uneasy rock. The springs squeaked and the seat groaned under his heavy load as he worked the chair back and forth with an ever-increasing frenzy. Suddenly, he lunged out of the chair and rammed the palm of his hand into the pointed console light.

Once, twice, three times. Blood spurted from his hand, covering the light, but the flashing refused to stop. The pain diverted some of his anger and Jackson returned to his chair, licking his wound. He was calmer, but the taste of his own blood reminded him how much he hated the little red bastard.

The light was out to get him; he was sure of that. It wanted to send his ass to some frozen post in Alaska, but

3

he wasn't going to let it. He hated the cold; it made his hands swell up and his feet itch.

He knew what people were saying; that he was cracking up, couldn't take the strain, nerves getting him. He even heard one of them say it was claustrophobia; as if they expected him to start foaming at the goddamn mouth or something.

He had made up his mind after the last time. If maintenance couldn't fix the light, he wasn't going to take the heat. No more false alarms, no more talk about pill popping, and no more shit from the colonel.

The sight of the empty chair across the room renewed his hatred for the system. He wasn't supposed to be alone. It wasn't supposed to be that way. Two men—that was the rule. The light never acted up unless he was alone, and he wasn't supposed to be alone. Where the hell was that replacement Roselli promised to send? Liar! Fuckin' liar. How do you report a superior to a superior without getting your ass kicked to Freezeburg. Fuck Roselli. Fuck Saxon. Fuck the red light. Fuck the whole damned project.

With that, Jackson swiveled his chair around until the back of his head faced the pulsating light. He put his feet up on another chair, grabbed a comic book from the desk, and relaxed. Nothing was going to ruin his night.

Christ, he thought, looking down at the comic. Fifty bucks. What a rip. But what the hell can a guy do when he's a hundred miles from Shitburg and two hundred feet underground?

The price revolved in his mind until he took a good look at the cover. A chill ran up his spine, and goose bumps crawled across the back of his neck at the sight of Superman flying through outer space. Concentrating on the vibrant colors, he ran his fingertips over them like a blind person reading braille. They were soothing and stimulating at the same time. First he touched the cool blues, then the hot reds; he escaped into his tranquil world of color.

A second red light blinked unnoticed as Jackson turned the page and stared at the first picture. Superman was plunging toward earth. The colors flashed across his eyes and saturated his mind until he became a part of the picture. Everything Superman felt, Jackson felt. Everything the Man of Steel saw, he saw. Their minds were as one. Jackson was Superman. A third red light blinked mutely.

Superman-Jackson smashed into the earth with a thunderous roar that drowned out the slight click of the door as it opened behind the corporal. In an instant, Superman-Jackson tunneled to the core of the earth and was fighting for his life. He was surrounded by the oranges and reds of molten lava. Intense heat pulled the breath from him. Sweat rolled down his neck.

Jackson's hands gripped the edges of the pages and his arms shot out to his sides, ripping the comic in two. The dry colors on the quivering pages were splattered with blood as Corporal Jackson's head was torn from his neck.

LIGHT FROM THE LIVING ROOM FILTERED UNDER THE BED-
room door, found its way to the bed, and glinted off the
metal object that should have been Colonel C. P. Saxon's
left arm. It was soft and pliable and yet as cold as death.
The arm pulsed with its own nuclear life. Even in his
sleep, the lethal gloved fingers clawed the air.

Saxon's six-foot-four-inch body lay bent and drawn
among the damp, tangled sheets; evidence of past convul-
sions and a forewarning of those to come lay with him. The
sweat-drenched muscles were hard and taut, waiting for the
pain.

Before the whirling, muddled images that filled his
mind could clear, even before his eyes opened, Saxon was
on his feet. With a gun in one hand and a chill throughout
his body, he faced the bedroom door and waited in the
dark. Thoughts ran through his head in a jumble. He tried
to catch one, to hold it long enough to see it clearly, but he
could only feel the sickening nausea that gripped his body.
He leaned heavily against the dresser and waited for the
chaos in his mind to subside as it had a hundred times
since the operation.

Bits and pieces of a dream floated in and out of his
grasp, staying just long enough to let him know it had been
with him that night. It was always the same. The cool
green of the steamy Mexican jungle mixed with sounds of

6

dying men. The rain, the mud, and the river. Saxon's river. Like a decaying serpent, it twisted and turned through the jungle, ending at Saxon's feet. It was his river, filled with the bodies of men he had put there.

The nightmare had become a welcomed friend; his only link with the rapidly fading past. Since the operation, his ability to remember had declined steadily. He was cut off from his past, and unsure of his future. Had he been a religious man, he would have thought he'd lost his soul.

All traces of the dream disappeared as the faint sound of breaking glass snapped him back to reality. He pushed away from the dresser and faced the door leading to the living room. He threw on his robe, careful to cover himself completely, and headed across the room. Gun in hand, he flung open the door and bolted into the living room.

Rita Baker sat curled up on the couch, a whisky bottle in one hand and a glass in the other. Her flaming red hair hung in ringlets about her sensuous face, and her deep green eyes flashed with excitement at the sight of Saxon's gun pointing at her.

"It's a very pretty gun," she said. "But it's not as big as the one you usually use."

She smiled, biting the tip of her tongue as she watched Saxon lower the gun. She waited for a response, but none came. She searched his face for some small sign that he was glad to see her—a smile, a slight grin, any emotion. There was none.

"Of course," she continued. "That was a long time ago." Pausing briefly, she looked down at his crotch and added teasingly, "Maybe you've lost it?"

Saxon didn't answer. He went to the wet bar, cleared away the broken glass, and poured himself a drink. She could see he was in a rage and it pleased her. It was a step. Uncoiling her long, slender legs, she rested one foot on the back of the couch, letting her dress slide to her hips.

"Hope I didn't disturb your sleep," she taunted.

Saxon whirled and caught the full effect of her pose. She ran her teeth across her bottom lip as she watched the bulge beneath his robe grow.

"Oh," she observed. "You haven't lost your—bazooka after all."

"How the hell did you get in?" Saxon demanded.

It was Rita's turn to not respond. She just fingered a gold chain that hung around her neck and slowly pulled up a key to his room from between her firm breasts. Saxon quickly crossed to the couch, grabbed the necklace, and ripped it from her. The chain bit into her neck, leaving a thin white line against her flawless skin.

"Next time knock!"

"Any particular place?" she asked, looking at the gold chain he held in the gloved hand. The beauty of the delicate gold chain against the rough black leather heightened her desire. It was the first time she had seen him use the artificial arm for anything. He usually let the arm hang at his side like so much dead weight. To have seen the arm actually move, to feel its fingers closing around her necklace, was something she never expected. She never took her eyes from it as Saxon circled around behind the couch.

"What the hell are you doing here, Rita?"

"I'm on official business."

"Tell me about it."

"I was chosen by the girls at Central to verify a rumor."

"Go on."

"Well, they were just wondering, because you haven't seen anyone at Central since the operation, if the rumor was true or not."

"What rumor?" Saxon demanded, gulping a large drink.

"That you've traded your bazooka for a handgun," Rita replied innocently.

Saxon choked on the drink. His huge frame shuddered. He leaned over the back of the couch and grabbed Rita by her throat. "I could kill you for that!" he threatened, holding her slender throat with his gloved hand.

Rita knew it was useless to try to break loose, even if she wanted to. She could feel the power of the hand and realized that he could snap her neck like a straw. She didn't move, didn't talk until he relaxed his grip.

"Well," she said seductively. "It wouldn't be the first time you've tried."

Saxon pulled her head up to his with a sudden jerk that left her dizzy. She parted her lips slightly as he brought his close to them. Then, just before they touched, he dropped her and went back to the bar. She sat up slowly, took a cigarette from her purse, and lit it. She let out the smoke and the question at the same time.

"Why?"

Saxon was on his third drink when he answered. "I'm tired of you! Don't you get the message?"

"And you're tired of Jan and Dee—and let's not forget Rose."

"Right!" Saxon said without turning away from the bar.

"Balls!" Rita snapped. "Your cock's about to bust and you expect me to believe that 'tired' shit?"

Saxon's speed stunned her as he rushed across the room, grabbed the back of the couch, and tipped it, dumping her on the floor.

"I expect you to get the hell out of here! I don't want your pity."

Rita's mouth had hit the coffee table. The salty taste of blood played between her teeth. She leaned towards Saxon, breasts straining against her dress with every quickened breath, her eyes meeting Saxon's steady glare. "Now that you've told me what you don't want, show me what you do want."

Saxon knelt over Rita, trapping her between his knees, grabbed her by the neck, and jerked her lips to his. Her tongue darted in and out of his consuming mouth as he pushed her back against the couch. His right hand searched the top of her dress for an opening.

"No," she said, pulling back. "This one."

Rita raised the gloved hand to her mouth and kissed its fingertips. She felt its power radiating through the leather as she bit the fingertips, slowly pulling the glove off with backward tugs of her head. As the glove slipped off, she saw the hand's highly polished Belium surface, shining like chrome, and was drawn to it. Cautiously, with one finger, she touched it.

"It's warm," she cried in amazement. Then, unable to control her desire, she pushed the hand down to the top of her dress and listened to the fabric tear as she sought to feel the warmth of the metal against her breasts. Wherever it touched, the hand set her afire with passion. It became the center of her consciousness, and dominated her every thought. When Saxon entered her, his lunging thrusts filled her very soul. At the height of her passion, Rita tore open Saxon's robe and saw the rough gray skin that extended from a seamless left shoulder joint to cover half his body. A wave of horror swept over her and, as Saxon's final violent thrusts plunged deep within her, she screamed.

THE CONSTANT POUNDING DRIFTED INTO MAJOR ROSELLI'S sleep like the ocean tide through a dense morning fog. It annoyed him and he fought it. He didn't know how long he had been asleep, but it sure as hell wasn't long enough. He knew if he could hold out, the sonofabitch would go away. He pulled a pillow down over his head, but it was too late. A quick glance at the bedside clock, and he was stumbling towards the door.

"I'm coming, damn it!" he shouted in an effort to stop the now frantic pounding. Whoever was on the other side of that door had better have a damn good reason or there'd be a real ass chewing. The thought consoled him as he fumbled with the lock and swung the door open.

"What the hell do you? . . ." He was stunned speechless at the sight of Rita Baker. Her dress was torn, and the usually curly hair hung in damp tangles about her mascara-streaked face. Before he could protest, she pushed past him into the room, leaving Roselli nervously checking the corridor to make sure no one had seen her enter. He quickly closed the door and turned in time to see Rita pour a drink and down it like so much distilled water. It took two more before her violently shaking hands calmed to a sporadic quiver.

"Are you out of your fuckin' mind?" Roselli asked.

Rita didn't answer. She knew if she tried to talk, there

11

would be a quaking in her voice. Roselli would take it as a sign of weakness and, like dealing with any wild animal, she knew that could be fatal. She used the time to take a good look at him. She couldn't recall the last time she'd seen him naked to the waist. She had trouble believing he was only six feet tall. Maybe it was the menacing way he always stood, as if waiting to spring into action. His hard muscles strained at his swarthy skin as he took a step towards her.

"I asked you a question, bitch!" Roselli shouted.

When Rita felt her control returning, she issued a tense answer. "It's Saxon." Her voice didn't crack, but her body still shuddered at the sound of his name. "I—just came from his room."

"You know how he plays. If it's too rough for you, stay away from him," Roselli replied coldly.

"No one plays too rough for me. Remember that!"

"I remember telling you not to come running back when Lover-Boy got tired of you, so get the hell out!"

Rita put her glass down and moved slowly towards the door. She had a secret, but before she revealed it, she wanted him to drop his guard. She wanted to see the expression on his face. Looking over her shoulder, she saw his smug smile and knew the time was right.

"Saxon's dead," she said calmly.

The smile disappeared, Roselli's jaw went slack, and his eyebrows arched. It was a disappointing display of shock. Then, just as she was about to lose all hope of getting to him, Roselli grabbed her arm and spun her around.

"What do you mean 'dead'?"

"D—E—A—D! As in 'no longer living.'"

"Are you sure?" His grip tightened on her arm.

"I know a dead man when I see one."

"Did you check his pulse? Maybe he just passed out."

"No pulse. No heartbeat. No breath. Nothing!"

Roselli relaxed his grip and she managed to pull free. The white imprints of his fingers were etched into her arm. Rita stepped back, but he closed the space between them.

"When?"

"A few minutes ago."

"Have you told anyone else?"

"You think I'm dumb or something? I'm not getting mixed up in it. Let somebody else find him."

"Right. Good thinking," Roselli said as he backed away. His comment took her by surprise. In the four years she had known Roselli, he had never once paid her the slightest compliment; not even when they were lovers. She rubbed her arm where he had held her, and watched him pace about the small room. She had forgotten how strong he was. Tucking a bottle of whisky under her arm, she sat on the couch and poured another drink, waiting for Roselli to stop moving around.

Roselli stopped in the middle of the room and stared at her. No, she thought, he wasn't staring at her, he was staring through her, his eyes focused on something in back of her. She looked around—a blank wall. He made her uneasy, she wasn't sure of what he was doing. Then it came to her: he was thinking. It had long been one of her beliefs that Roselli didn't know how to think, but there he was doing it.

"We'll have to stop," Roselli said, beginning to pace again.

"Why?" Rita questioned. "With Saxon dead, you'll be head of Security and things will be easier."

"Headquarters won't promote me. I'm as far up the ladder as I'm going to get. As soon as they find out Saxon's dead, they'll send a replacement—some tight-assed shit afraid for his job and he'll clamp down so hard you'll need a pass to piss."

"How long do we stop for?" Rita asked anxiously, sitting forward on the edge of the couch and putting the bottle of whisky and her glass down on the table.

"How should I know? Maybe a couple months—maybe forever."

"What about the bets we have?"

"The next few days will take care of them. With all the red tape and ass kissing that'll be going on, it'll take at least that long before the replacement gets here. With any luck, Saxon won't be found until late tomorrow, maybe even the day after—that would be better."

"Don't count on it," Rita said firmly. "Someone's bound to notice he's missing and go looking for him."

"Not that sonofabitch. No one's going to look for trouble. Unless," Roselli glared at her, "they've got a hot cunt! And according to rumor, even that wouldn't be a reason for scratching on Saxon's door."

Rita sat on the couch, ignoring the jabs, and watched as Roselli dug a thick notebook out from behind a dresser and headed for the bathroom.

"Are you going to destroy it?"

"No, I'm going to turn myself in," he said sarcastically.

Rita followed him into the bathroom and sat on the toilet while he began tearing pages from the book and dropping them in the bathtub.

"What about the smoke alarm?"

Without answering, Roselli reached up to the low ceiling and ripped off the small sensor. When the pile of paper reached a workable height, he closed the door and reached for a match in his pants pocket, then realized he only had on underwear. He stormed from the small room abruptly, muttering something about there being an international plot to screw Roselli.

The sounds of cussing and banging drawers floated back to Rita as she glanced up at a matchless Roselli bolting back into the bathroom.

"Got a match?"

"No," she lied, enjoying his panic.

After several more minutes of drawer banging, Roselli reappeared with a crumpled matchbook containing two equally crumpled matches.

"Nothing ever works out for me," he complained as he bent low over the mound of paper bets and watched the first match fizzle. "Sonofabitching goddamn bastard," he shouted down at the match. He spun the matchbook around in his hand, trying to locate a manufacturer's name—none. "Nothing works for me," he muttered as he plucked out the last match.

Rita didn't feel like listening to any more drawers bang, so she took the match, struck it, and lit the pile of paper in several places. She returned to her seat while Roselli plucked out more pages from the shrinking book, adding them to the growing flames.

"Big fucking deal," he shouted. "A couple of thousand a week. What do they expect people to do for entertainment?" He clasped his hands on his scalp with quick jerking motions accompanied by the sounds of frustration. He looked at Rita's stone face—no sympathy there—and continued.

"You can't put people underground like goddamn moles and expect them to watch reruns of kiddie cartoons on a goddamn closed-circuit TV," he continued. "I'm providing a goddamn service, for Christ's sake. Don't they realize that? I should get a goddamn medal or something. People got social needs. No wonder everyone's going out of their goddamn heads!"

"Talking about social needs," Rita began. "Some of the girls from Central are still using your name for protection."

"Jesusss!" Roselli exclaimed. "Now, I'm a goddamn pimp!" He ran his hands over his clean-shaven head. "Someone sneaks in porno films—I'm the source. Another creep brings in dope—I'm the pusher. If there's a card game, I'm the dealer! Where's the fucking money? I'm being set up as the biggest fall guy in the whole fucking world—and I can't even pay my fucking alimony!"

Rita wasn't listening. Her mind was back on the 'couple thousand a week' statement. "Why am I only getting two hundred a week if you're making two thousand?"

"That's gross," Roselli explained. "Out of that I've got expenses and losses and depreciation and—"

"And you're a goddamn liar!" Rita shouted. The look in Roselli's eyes told her her timing was lousy. When she left the bathroom, he was right behind her. She heard his footsteps stop as she crossed the living room towards the front door.

"Where do you think you're going?" Roselli asked.

Rita didn't turn around, but kept walking. "You said yourself we shouldn't be seen together." She didn't hear him coming after her, so she thought she was safe until she reached for the door. His fingers wrapped around her arm, spinning her across the room and over the back of the couch. He was on her like a great cat, pinning her down and enjoying her helplessness.

"You should've thought about that before," he said. "Now that you're here, you might as well stay awhile." His hand caught the top of her dress, ripping it to her waist. "It's time you paid for waking me up." His mouth closed on hers as his hot hands clutched at her round breasts. Rita grimaced in pain. She felt his hand slip from her breast and force her thighs apart.

She felt like she was suffocating. Roselli's tongue was relentlessly probing every corner of her mouth. It was not new to her. His technique had never changed during the year they were lovers. His attack was always violent, but short lived. Her one chance was to divert his attention, which wouldn't be hard to do if she could talk. She played her part by struggling just enough so he wouldn't get mad. He needed that. He wanted to rape and conquer. She would wait for phase two.

Roselli withdrew his tongue, sucked her tongue into his mouth, and held it there with his teeth. Rita winced from the old familiar pain—it was the beginning of his second phase of love. When he released her tongue and buried his teeth into her left nipple, she yelled at him.

"Make it a good fuck. You'll need to remember it for a long time."

It never ceased to amaze her how Roselli could be turned off like a light bulb. He pulled back, looked puzzled, and released her.

"What are you talking about?"

"Saxon's arm."

"His artificial arm?"

"Yeah, only it's not so artificial anymore. The damn thing grew to him. There's no joint." She still couldn't sit up, but she was making progress.

Roselli sat on the edge of the couch thinking. He still had his hand up her dress, and his finger up her.

"I don't believe it," Roselli said, removing his hand from her and wiping his finger on her dress.

"Listen, you know he only had one arm when he first

came here. They should've kicked him out of the army, but they wanted him here—for some awful experiment—"

"Belium," Roselli interjected.

"And something went wrong. That Belium stuff is what this project's all about, isn't it?"

If Roselli had been less worried about his own ass, he would never have discussed top-secret matters like Belium. "Not anymore," he replied absentmindedly. "First was poison gas, then Belium, then . . ." He stopped short.

"Then what?" Rita pressed. "I've been on this project four years and I still don't know what it's about."

"If you know what's good for you, you'll forget what I just said."

"All right, all right. But here's something I can't forget. Half of Saxon's body was covered with dark crud. His skin looked like it was charred with a blowtorch."

Rita had hardly finished speaking when Roselli got up and started pacing again. She took the opportunity to fix her dress as best she could and slide over the back of the couch. Roselli caught her halfway to the door.

"Naughty, naughty," he said, twisting her arm.

"Let me go," Rita pleaded. "When Saxon's found, there'll be investigators crawling all over this place. I thought you'd be in a position to cover it up, but you won't. Don't you see?"

"I won't have to cover it up, the doctors will. They warned Saxon there might be some staining."

"It wasn't just stain. It felt like he was ramming a steel rod up me," said Rita, struggling to get away.

"That shouldn't bother you," Roselli said, pulling her up a little more and smiling as she winced.

"I sure as hell never had to worry about that with you," Rita said.

Roselli slapped her across the mouth, sending her sprawling across the floor. Catching her by the hair, he jerked her up.

"Listen good, bitch! Saxon's arm is classified. Everything you saw or felt is classified. Just knowing about it can get you ten years on a trumped-up spy charge. Talking about it can get you twenty more." Tired of her fingernails digging into his hands, he tossed her back on the couch.

"Bastard!"

"Shut your mouth. There will be an investigation. Nothing big—just for show—and that'll be it. But, if you try to run, they'll be on your ass before you can get out the door. They'll want the right answers, and you won't have them."

"What you really mean is you're afraid they'll find out I've been laying off some of the heavy bets through Central and they'll trace them back to you."

The knife seemed to come from nowhere. One second his hands were empty, the next he had a switchblade. To Rita, it looked like the end of a perfect evening.

"And if they catch me because of something you do . . ." Roselli emphasized his message by jerking her up off the couch and pressing the knife against her throat.

Roselli's expression went numb as he felt the boxcar unload on his balls. He doubled over. Rita's knee caught him in the face, smashing him backwards to the floor. He lay dazed against the dresser, barely able to hear.

"Rita baby is getting out, and not with that fucking ten percent you've been handing out. I want half or I go straight to Headquarters. By the time I'm finished 'talking' with the brass, they'll be sure I'm an innocent victim."

Roselli opened his eyes to a spinning room and seventeen Ritas. As the room began to slow, he gripped the knife and made a feeble lunge at her. Rita's foot smashed into his jaw, and blood gushed into his mouth.

"You've got till noon. Then, little Rita will get the little men from Headquarters to hang you by your little balls."

Roselli lay on the floor watching Rita pause in her exit in front of the full-length mirror. The last thing he heard before he slipped into unconsciousness was Rita swearing.

"Damn, this was my favorite dress."

```
TIME     :  2332
AREA     :  DR. RICEMAN'S ROOM
LEVEL    :  1
SENSORS  :  301–3
```

"ARE YOU GOING TO DO SOMETHING ABOUT IT OR NOT?"

Michelle Montignac finished the question as she reached the center of the small room and turned abruptly towards Doctor Benjamin Riceman.

He looked at her tall lean body and wished she would forget about secret experiments and clandestine meetings and hidden forces. It had been the same old story since she had arrived to replace his old assistant, Hubert, a year ago.

"If you had some evidence—" he was cut short by the tossing of Michelle's head in a decidedly disgusted manner. He wondered if he still had a chance of getting her into bed.

"Why do you find it so hard to believe?" she asked. "If you told me that you could make a metal that was as flexible as human skin and indestructible, I'd believe you. I'd take your word for it."

"Would you?" Riceman countered.

Michelle thought about it. That was another thing he liked about her. She didn't just give an answer because it would help her argument. She aimed for the truth.

"All right. Maybe I wouldn't believe you," she admitted. "But I'd give you the right to be wrong. I'd listen—at least that."

He wanted to tell her he was sick of listening—had been listening for months that seemed years. He didn't want to

19

listen anymore; he didn't want to talk. He wanted to ravage her slinky body in a kindly manner. All five feet ten inches of it, six even, in her heels. He liked heels, spiked mostly. Black. With black silk stockings. He knew it was out of style, but he couldn't help it. That's the way he was raised. He could comb his hair differently, but not his brain. As he looked across at her split skirt, her legs seemed seven yards long. . . .

"You aren't going to even *try* to do anything about it are you?" she accused.

He liked it when she yelled. Her long-lipped mouth parted like red curtains to reveal snapping teeth white as porcelain. Maybe if he didn't answer, she'd yell again.

"You think you're the smartest man in the world!" she yelled. White porcelain snapping. "Know everything—can't learn anything from a stupid woman."

Riceman loved it when she talked forcefully. He wondered if now would be a good time to kiss her. She wouldn't be able to talk—he wouldn't have to listen—he could ravage her slinky body in a kindly manner.

"Say something!" she ordered, her small, sculptured fist shaking at him—shaking the right side of her torso—making her heavy breasts swing freely under her blouse.

Riceman crossed to Michelle slowly, the half smile on his face set solid by the snapping porcelain and shaking fist. He took her in his arms and dipped her slinky body. The red curtains were now wide with surprise. Instead of lips, he kissed her porcelains. He lost his balance and crashed thunderously on top of her. The romance of the moment lost in the numbing clatter of their teeth.

They were two cement statues on the floor. Michelle's sable eyes had turned hard with shock. His mud brown peepers had frozen to a glassy stare. He hoped she wouldn't make a totally big deal out of this mess.

Between clinched teeth, Michelle shouted, "What are you doing?"

Riceman wanted to say, 'nothing,' in hopes she hadn't noticed his hand on her breast. His left arm was stuck under her back, his right hand glued to her silk-covered breast in fear any move would be taken by her as a definite grope.

Michelle shouted her question again, this time adding a remark about his sanity. As he was searching for an answer, the phone rang.

"Excuse me," he said, suddenly rolling off her. "The phone's ringing."

Michelle rolled to one side, and freed his arm, allowing him to catch the phone on the fourth ring. The message was short, but he carried on the dead conversation in hopes that he might distract her.

"Sure thing," he said as he heard the end to Michelle's shuffling. He slammed down the phone in mock anger, trying hard not to show any sign of relief.

"Computer's down again," he explained. "Back in a minute."

Riceman raced out the door before Michelle had a chance to protest.

TIME	:	2336
AREA	:	COLONEL C. P. SAXON'S QUARTERS
LEVEL	:	1
SENSORS	:	431–32; 434–35; 1187*

THE THIN LAYER OF ICE COVERING SAXON'S BODY SLOWLY melted and rose from him in a grayish mist as the room's temperature returned to normal. Light seeped through his glazed eyes, cutting into his brain like a hot knife. It was his only sensation of life, and he clung to the searing pain with the desperation of a drowning man. Like a great paralyzed knight entombed in a suit of armor, he lay peering out of the eyeholes, waiting for death.

An explosion deep in his chest rocked his entire body. Sporadic explosions followed one after another until they became a steady beat, and Saxon finally recognized the sound of his own heart. The hiss of rushing air followed quickly, as his massive chest began to move. His eyelids twitched, then closed, shielding him from the torturous light.

The burning pain was replaced by a deadly cold that engulfed his entire body. He felt as though ice water was coursing through his veins. As the feeling spread through-

* SENSOR 1187 RECORDED A DROP IN TEMPERATURE THAT BEGAN AT 2314 HOURS AND CONTINUED UNTIL 2333 HOURS. AT ITS LOWEST POINT, THE ROOM REACHED −23° FAHRENHEIT. THERE WERE NO INDICATIONS OF A MALFUNCTION OF THE THERMOSTAT.

out his body, so did his ability to move, and he found himself standing unsteadily in the middle of the room.

Remembering the pain of the light, Saxon opened his eyes cautiously. Yet there was no torture, just the sensation of looking through tinted glasses. He wondered how long he had been out. From his position, he could see the L.E.D. clock in the bedroom. But, at that distance, the red numerals blended into one bright red mass. All he could think about was the time, and not being able to read the clock. His hatred grew for the shaky legs that kept him from walking into the bedroom; he hated the cold that gripped his body; and he hated the damn clock that blurred before him. Suddenly, the red numerals separated, cleared, and became distinct. It was 2344.

The first step towards the bedroom was the hardest. A numbness in his legs made it seem like walking on stilts. One step followed another until Saxon was making erratic progress through the bedroom door. Once he reached the bed, he collapsed, catching himself on the side of it and then falling backwards to the floor.

Grabbing the corner of the dresser, he pulled himself up to his feet. Even in the near total darkness of the room, Saxon caught a glimpse of himself in the dresser mirror, and the shock forced him to his knees. There, for the first time in his life, he cried. He cried for all the things he could have been, and for all the things he would be. It was the last time he felt the least remorse for the course he had chosen; and the last time he ever questioned his duty.

As he got to his feet again, he turned on the ceiling of light and looked down at his body. The skin was dark, cracked, unreal to his touch. His feet had not changed, but he could tell by the spreading gray cancer reaching down to his ankles that he didn't have long to wait. The same was true of his right hand. He looked in the mirror. His face would take longer. The transformation was just below his neck. Maybe an hour, two at the most. It was happening faster than he had planned.

He pulled a knife from the dresser drawer, grabbed the handle with both hands, and thrust the blade into his heart;

the knife skidded across his chest without even leaving a mark.

For a moment, Saxon reveled in the thought of being indestructible. Nothing could stop him, not now. Then, in one of his few remaining moments of sanity, he remembered his neck and head. If someone shot him there, everything he had waited for would be gone. He was still vulnerable. A few more hours and he could do anything, be anything, and no one could stop him.

The shrill ring of the phone jolted Saxon from his glory. As he picked up the phone, his mind fought the return to reality.

"Saxon here!" he barked. The pause on the other end of the line indicated that his displeasure had been duly noted.

"Lieutenant Brenner, sir. We have a Factor Seven security breech," the voice said defensively.

"Let's have it!" Saxon ordered.

"We've lost contact with Security Control on Level Four."

"Phone lines again?"

"Yes, sir. But that's not all."

Saxon waited for further explanation, but all he heard was silence. "Are you going to tell me, Brenner, or do you want me to guess?"

"Sorry, sir. BRUCE went down hard just after midnight. As always, whenever there's computer trouble, we reverted to a manual mode and I started calling Level Four Security Control every ten minutes."

"And what did Major Roselli have to say?"

"I didn't talk to the major, sir. Corporal Jackson answered the phone."

"Every time?"

"Yes, sir."

"You never talked to the major?"

"No, sir."

"Go on."

"Corporal Jackson said everything was okay. No problems."

"But you didn't believe him?"

"Oh, I believed him. I've known the corporal several years and I trust his judgment."

"Let me get this straight. You had a routine computer breakdown, followed by routine phone calls to the Level Four Security Control area during which Corporal Jackson routinely told you that everything was all right, followed by a routine phone-line breakdown. Is that about it, Private Brenner?" Saxon asked sarcastically.

"Lieutenant Brenner, sir," Brenner corrected. "That's not all, there's more."

"I can hardly wait," Saxon mocked. "But I have the feeling I'll have to."

"As you know, sir," Lieutenant Brenner began, "Security Procedure 443 requires that all phone communications be verified by running a voiceprint check."

"For God's sake," Saxon yelled, unable to contain his frustration any longer, "don't tell me what I already know. I wrote the goddamn book! Get to the point!"

"I couldn't run the check when I was talking to Jackson because the computer was down. So I routinely," the word stuck in Brenner's throat, "recorded his voice and ran it through BRUCE when the system came up. That was about four minutes ago."

"And?"

"It didn't check. I know Jackson's voice when I hear it, and that was Jackson. Besides, I asked him about his family and all kinds of shit—excuse me, sir—all kinds of things, and it was definitely him."

"But it didn't check out."

"That's right, sir."

"Did you do a scan?"

"Yes, sir. And that's another thing. The voice didn't match anything—"

"Maybe there's something wrong with your recorder."

"I don't think so, sir. I even thought there was something wrong with BRUCE, what with being down and all. So I recorded my voice and ran it through and it checked out."

"Were you able to contact Jackson after the negative check?"

"No, sir. The phone lines went down just before BRUCE came up."

"What's your conclusion, lieutenant?"

"I was hoping you'd have one, sir."

"Send down a security team."

"I did, sir. We tracked them until they got off the elevator. We couldn't get a fix on them through the Level Four shield. They haven't reported back. Funny thing is one of them was supposed to stay on the elevator and keep in constant radio contact with us, but they all got off. What do you make of it?"

"There's a high probability Level Four has been contaminated. Activate emergency procedure Island. This is not a drill, lieutenant. Do you understand?"

"Yes, sir."

"Don't wait for me. Do it now!"

```
TIME     :  2356
AREA     :  CORRIDORS A21; F7; W13
LEVEL    :  1
SENSORS  :  21–25; 77–81; 133
```

"SHIT!" SAXON MUTTERED AS HE LEFT HIS QUARTERS. "Seven fucking minutes." It had taken longer to get dressed than he figured. His coordination was coming back, but not fast enough. He was glad the corridor was empty. No one would see him limping along; a man fighting for control over his own body.

It took all his concentration just to propel himself down the hall without falling. He wasn't used to that. He had always been in top shape, able to make his body do whatever he wanted. Turning into Corridor F, he lost his balance and fell against the wall. In frustration, he drove his fist through it.

Withdrawing his hand from the hard plaster, he looked at the gaping hole. He had only meant to pound on the wall, but the gloved hand had sliced through it with unbelievable ease. As adrenaline surged through his veins, a feeling of unparalleled power flooded him—a power he wouldn't hesitate to use.

He looked again at the corridors. Where were the guards? That sonofabitch Brenner hadn't activated Island. What was taking so long?

Suddenly there was an earsplitting rumbling overhead. The floor shook and twisted, toppling Saxon like a toy soldier. By the time he got to his feet, the once empty corri-

dor was filled with running, pushing people. The wail of
the sirens mixed with their terrified cries. The lights flickered and plunged them into a nightmarish void of total
darkness. Saxon fought to stay upright, knowing one slip
could be his last.

He couldn't see them, but he could feel them pressing
against him from all sides until he was drowning in a sea of
liquid humanity. He covered his ears to escape the unbear-
able noise. Their body heat swept over him, filling his
lungs and suffocating him. He opened his mouth in a desperate effort to breathe. In that instant, he knew. He saw.
He remembered jungles of Mexico, and the snakes that
hunted at night, and the infrared cameras that turned heat
into pictures. Wherever he turned his head, heat filled his
mouth, transforming itself into images. Waving forms of
faint red, but images all the same.

They were in terror then too. In hoards, they swam the
river in a desperate escape from the Magic Dragon, its
breath sweeping the black jungle into a rage of fire.

His men met them on the high bank, held them back
against the broiling heat—against the flaming tongue
flying silently above.

Saxon's men held the bank. Four against two hundred,
but they held. Each with a machine gun, each turning the
dark waters into a crimson eruption. And when it was over,
when the last shriek had cut through the night, Saxon
turned his weapon on the last four of his men.

Two hundred and four Rangers who had ruled the jungle for three years. They were killers in a time when killers
were needed. Their vicious savagery had turned the war.
But, like mad dogs, they could never go home. Home was
afraid . . .

As the floor shook again, the memory of promises given
and broken, of endless reassignments around the world,
spewed into Saxon's dark mind. Memories of ten years belowground, of waiting for a handshake that never came,
drove Saxon to the edge of madness. Bodies fell as he
struck out in all directions, pushing his way upstream towards Security Command.

They had kept him belowground. Like a fearful thing best forgotten. A distasteful bit of history. A nightmare.

Tonight he would be going home. And if they were afraid of him, they had a right to be. . . .

```
TIME     :   0003  12 JANUARY 1998*
AREA     :
LEVEL    :
SENSORS  :
```

---

* 0003–0011. NO RECORDS AVAILABLE. PROBABLE CAUSE: MALFUNCTION OF RECORDING SYSTEM.

TIME	:	0012
AREA	:	OUTSIDE SECURITY COMMAND
LEVEL	:	1
SENSORS	:	142

"54317," RICEMAN REPEATED. NOTHING. HE GAVE IT A FEW more seconds, but the large red door didn't open. "I said 543—"

"I heard you," the speaker over the door shouted. "I'm not deaf."

"Just dumb," Riceman accused.

"Name calling won't get us anywhere," the metallic voice condescended. "I'm *just* the computer. You're the hotshot programmer. It's obvious you didn't fix the problem."

Riceman kicked the door. "It's obvious you're being a shithead! Everyone in the whole goddamn place can get in but me."

"That's not true."

"It is true," Riceman shouted. "And I'll tell you something else. You're not only a shithead, you're a pompous asshole—and—and no one wants to communicate with you anymore!"

"That's a lie!" the speaker crackled.

"Ever since you got that Molecular Memory, you've been a real bastard," Riceman accused. "I've tried to help you. God knows I've tried. But you won't be helped. Well, I'm through. Finished."

"You're just saying that to cheer me up."

Riceman's mud-dark eyes flashed and his thick sandy

31

hair shook as he took the computer manual he was carrying and slammed it against the wall.

"Read the damn thing yourself!"

He knew throwing a manual against a wall was an irrational thing to do, but it did seem to give him a temporary sense of accomplishment. The fact was, it made him feel so good, he considered doing it again. Just pick up the manual and slap-bang it again. And again, if he felt like it. Why not?

No one would notice. Everyone had been running around in near panic since the earthquake and a little more noise would be lost in the din of hysteria. One look at the bug-eyed-wild herd made Riceman wish the emergency lights had never come on.

He had managed to get to the computer library because the river was flowing in that direction; getting back was another matter. If the crowd hadn't stopped like a huge traffic jam, he would never have been able to fight his way back. Now, looking at the crumpled manual on the floor, he wondered if he had done the right thing.

People were jamming up at the exits, so that meant the hallways to his room—to Michelle—were probably empty. He resisted the urge to check on her. She was probably at her post anyway, or on her way to it. Everyone had specific orders to follow during an emergency. Riceman was trying to remember his.

"Let's get inside."

The voice was that of Colonel Saxon. Riceman looked up in time to see him kick a well-worn place on the wall beside the red door. The door slid open and both men disappeared through the opening.

```
TIME     :  0015
AREA     :  SECURITY COMMAND
LEVEL    :  1
SENSORS  :  001–18
```

SAXON TOOK A FEW STEPS INSIDE THE DOOR AND STOPPED. Riceman, looking back at the door as it slid shut, caromed off Saxon like a tennis ball off a concrete wall.

The sixty-seven security personnel were standing in the center of the room staring up at a blank videoscreen. An air of reverence hung over them like a heavy cloak. Except for the few muffled sounds of hardened men trying to hold back their emotions, the only noise was the click of computer console keys. Saxon's first urge was to bust through the crowd and get some answers, but he held back. Something was going on that required a different approach.

"What's wrong with them?" Riceman asked. "Haven't they ever been in an earthquake before?"

"Sir?" Saxon heard someone call from across the room. It was Lieutenant Brenner, working his way through the crowd. He was red-faced and pale at the same time, like some circus clown. His left eye twitched sporadically. Saxon recognized the twitch as a sure sign of bad news. As usual, Brenner stopped in front of Saxon and gave a proper salute.

"Has the surface phoned down with a damage report?" Saxon asked without returning Brenner's salute.

"No, sir," Brenner answered, maintaining the salute.

There was no way out of it, Saxon would have to give a half-assed salute before Brenner would relax. He had seen

Brenner stand like that for twenty minutes, just sweating and waiting. Saxon brushed his hair out of his eyes, and Brenner accepted the movement as a salute.

"Thank you, sir."

"Get to it, lieutenant," Saxon ordered. "What did Surface say happened up there?"

"Nothing, sir."

"They said nothing happened?"

"No, sir. I meant they haven't said anything. We have no reason to believe that—" Brenner was having a hell of a time reporting to Saxon. Almost as if his findings wouldn't be real if he didn't say them out loud.

"What the hell's going on!" Saxon demanded.

"Everything's gone, sir. Murdock is getting it up on the screen now. We've lost all contact with the surface. All the video monitors and almost all the sensors—gone. There was an explosion—you'll see. It's recorded. Murdock is getting—"

"That's enough, lieutenant. I get the idea. Don't jump to conclusions. Let's get a computer analysis of what the sensors recorded."

"The printers are down. Not physically. BRUCE just won't talk to them, and we can't get the dumps we need on video, there's just too much."

"How about a summary?"

"Sure, we can get that. Some of the discpacks went off line during the shake, and we haven't got 'em back yet. Montignac is working the problem. She's real good. Shouldn't take long."

Riceman had been right. Michelle had gone to her data-storage post. He looked toward the rear of the large room—nothing. She was probably sitting at her desk behind the banks of discpacks. He took a step in that direction, then decided he'd better stick around Saxon awhile and see what all the fuss was about.

"While we're waiting," Saxon began, "you can tell me what happened to Island."

"It wouldn't activate, sir. BRUCE wouldn't take the instruction—kept giving back an error."

They turned and glared at Riceman. What did they want him to do about it? If BRUCE baby fucked up, they sure as hell weren't going to lay it at his feet. Island wasn't his ball park. Security. Top secret. He didn't even know what Island was supposed to do except shut off a few circuits, and some other things that had never been made clear. Besides, Mother handles that one herself. Updates the Island program directly from satellite to BRUCE baby. Never touches human hands.

"I wasn't here," Riceman explained.

"That's true," Brenner confirmed to Saxon. "Doctor Riceman had gotten BRUCE up, then went to get a manual. That's when I called you, sir. I tried to activate Island, but BRUCE kicked the instruction out, saying something about it being illegal as long as ZOMBIE is in control of the system. Whatever the hell ZOMBIE is?" He looked again at Riceman.

"Never heard of it."

"Obviously something's still wrong with BRUCE," Saxon lied with a tone that put an end to the discussion.

Brenner followed him to the center of the room, where Murdock was working feverishly on a computer terminal muttering to himself about the piss-poor software and the piss-poor hardware and the piss—he smiled. He looked around once to make sure every eye was on him, pushed one last key, and slumped back in his chair. The large screen in the center of the room lit up with a tranquil scene of the camp as seen from a remote camera on one of the many gun towers.

"It's coming," Brenner announced solemnly. "I was watching when it happened—there, the shadow in the lower left—about seven o'clock—see?"

Saxon moved a little closer to the screen and watched the shadow dart from building to building until it reached the Belium tower in the center of the compound. The tower was typical of all gas towers: a relatively small column leading up to a large sphere that held the gas. Kind of like a golf ball on a tee. The shadow disappeared in the column for less than a minute, reappeared, and raced off towards the electrified fence that surrounded the compound. It broke through the fence as if it wasn't there, and disappeared into the desert.

"What was it?" the lieutenant asked, not really expecting an answer.

"I don't know," Saxon lied. "Maybe the tower cameras got a better shot of it."

"That's the only shot you're gonna get," Murdock explained. "Everything else was erased when BRUCE went down. I was only able to get that because there's a secondary recorder we're testing, and I was playing around with it and—you don't know what the hell I'm talking about; that's all there is."

"Watch the tower—anytime now . . ." Brenner warned.

He just finished when the Belium tower blew. What they had heard about a Belium blast was true. It didn't blow like a bomb, it mushroomed in a slow ball of fire. It was like watching slow motion, with everything else moving at regular speed. The fireball was preceeded by a severe heat wave that blew buildings apart like they were made of cardboard.

The camera was only two hundred yards from the tower, but it took the ball of fire over three minutes to reach it. In those three minutes, Saxon witnessed the death of close to five hundred people. Men and women ran from the buildings, their clothes on fire, and rolled on the ground in agony until the fireball covered them. Some ran wildly into the electric fence, choosing a quick death. The last thing the camera saw was a wall of flame coming at it.

The screen went blank, but no one moved. No one talked. They kept staring at the screen, expecting a TV announcer would tell them the show had been brought to them by Ford, or Kelloggs . . .

"What the hell was that?"

Saxon turned at the sound of the familiar voice and saw Major Roselli limping across the floor. When Saxon stepped from the crowd, Major Roselli froze.

"Where in the hell have you been?" Saxon asked.

"I . . ." Roselli couldn't answer, he was visibly shaken.

He took several steps toward Saxon to make sure he was seeing right. Convinced that Saxon was really there, he managed an answer. "Must've hit my head on something." He rubbed his head and took a closer look at Saxon.

"You should be more careful," Saxon warned. "That could be fatal."

"Don't worry about it," Roselli assured him. "I can take care of myself."

Without acknowledging Roselli's reply, Saxon turned to Brenner. "Lieutenant."

"Yes, sir," Brenner called as he crossed the room.

"The major and I are going to my office. I'll expect that damage report in—ten minutes."

With that and six strides, Saxon was out the door, followed by a reluctant Roselli and an uninvited but curious Riceman.

THEY WERE MET BY A MOB OF ANGRY AND CONFUSED PEOple in the corridor. Riceman was immediately separated from Saxon and Roselli, and squeezed out the back of the crowd. From his position, he could see the mass of clutching hands reaching out to Saxon.

Most of the shouts were lost in the garbled rush of incoherent questions. But there were a few questions that seemed to come from several people at the same instant, and so rose above the din.

"What's wrong with the elevators?"

"Why can't we get out the exits?"

"Was that an earthquake?"

Saxon's reply was silence and a stern look as he plowed through the crowd. Roselli had less success. Cornered and unable to break away, he used the diplomacy that had thus far marked his career.

"There's been an accident on the surface. And, because of that accident, none of you will have to pay any income tax this year."

"Why's that?" a voice in the back of the crowd asked over the puzzled silence.

"Because," Roselli smiled cruelly, "all you fucking idiots are going to die."

The shock stunned the crowd. They offered no resis-

38

tance as Roselli broke through them into the corridor behind Saxon.

Riceman, on the opposite side of the crowd, watched Saxon and Roselli disappear around a corner; Roselli's sadistic answer still rang in his ears, not that Riceman really cared one way or the other.

He had known for some time that he was going to live the rest of his life among the buried living, so it didn't matter to him that the elevators weren't working and the exits were blocked. No one had ever been able to get to the surface using one of them anyway. But the thought of impending death was fascinating. Rather than feeling panicked, he felt a strange tranquility.

His only worry was the way Michelle might take the news. He wanted to be the one to break it to her—gently. He would hate to see her end up like those raving maniacs, running around the corridors lamenting the end of this wonderful life.

He backed away from the crowd slowly, careful not to draw attention to himself or the goddamn red uniform he was wearing. If they saw that, they just might go for his throat, and he sure as hell wasn't a Saxon or even a Roselli.

Mobs, he reasoned, were unpredictable mainly because they were composed of people, and everyone knows how unpredictable people are. Since this mob showed no signs of breaking up, Riceman decided to head for his room.

He was not good in emergencies. Never had been. As he moved through the corridors, he thought about the time he ran into the street to save a dog and spent the rest of the summer in a youth hospital. He remembered jumping into a swimming pool to save a little girl and how mad the lifeguard was when he dragged Riceman from the water. He remembered how sleepy he had been afterward, and how sleepy he was now . . .

Sleep had become one of his favorite activities during the last several months. There never seemed to be enough. Sometimes he dreamed about sleeping. But it was the other dreams that worried him, the ones filled with lost details; they hung in his mind like shadows . . .

ROSELLI WAS STILL SMILING WHEN HE ENTERED SAXON'S office, but he didn't smile for long. Saxon whirled on him, hit him full force on the chest with the palm of his hand, and sent Roselli crashing against the wall. His head smashed into a picture, shattered the glass, and left a broken trail of blood down the wall as he slumped to the floor. Although taken by surprise and dazed by a blow that would have killed a lesser man, Roselli still managed to pull his revolver before he hit the floor.

"I should kill you," Saxon said, paying as much heed to the gun as he would a water pistol.

There was something in Saxon's eyes that warned Roselli that his life hung in a balance. A cold, numbing ache tore at his chest; in the split second he had been hit, the warmth in his chest had been sucked from him by Saxon's hand. It was like touching liquid nitrogen. Sweat glistened down the back of his neck, and he could barely feel the life returning to his lungs. He kept his gun pointed at Saxon's heart.

"Go on shoot!" Saxon taunted. "Or do you want me to get closer so you won't miss?"

In those few seconds before Roselli holstered his gun, Saxon saw a glimpse of the man known as the Black Reaper during the Oregon Police Action.

"Someday," Roselli warned, "you'll push too far!"

"I haven't started to push," Saxon snapped, taking a menacing step forward. "You were supposed to be on Level Four tonight!"

"The hell I was. McIntosh was number two! I traded with him."

"McIntosh has smoke for brains! He couldn't find his way to the john."

"He doesn't have to!" Roselli shouted. "We're all sitting on one big toilet and anytime Mother wants she can flush us and there's nothing we can do about it!"

Saxon smiled. "Mother has activated ZOMBIE."

Roselli's face drained white. "Why?"

"I don't know—not for sure," Saxon confessed. "But it started on Level Four. I think there was something in those cylinders and it got out."

Roselli had never believed in the project, but if ZOMBIE had been activated someone believed. He looked closely at Saxon. Maybe Rita was right after all.

"Phone lines out?" Roselli asked.

"Everything's out between floors. If the surface antennas are gone, we've lost communication with Mother too."

"Out hell," Roselli countered. "She's got sensors in every fucking wall. She may not be able to hear us now, but after this whole thing's over, she'll dig up that goddamn black box and have the biggest goddamn bang party this fucking country has ever seen!" Roselli hated the thought of a group of faceless snobs listening to "death tapes" while fucking faceless secretaries. "You say there's a rat loose in the basement. What's it going to do? Eat its fucking way up here?" He gave an uneasy laugh.

"Two rats. You saw one on the screen. There were two cylinders."

"Maybe the other one's up there too."

"That's what we're going to find out."

"How?"

"We've got to defuse ZOMBIE. To do that, we've got to get Riceman to Level Four. That's how we'll find out."

"He won't go—not even if you threaten to kill him. He's just waiting to die anyway; he sure as hell won't work at it."

"Leave him to me," Saxon ordered. "He'll go willingly. You just make sure he gets down there in one piece!"

"If you think I'm volunteering for a mission like that, you're out of your fucking mind—sir!"

Saxon got up and leaned over the desk. "You've got a choice to make. You can take your chances down there, or you can die right here!"

Saxon shoved the desk aside and was on him before Roselli could clear his gun. The shot went through the bottom of his chair, richocheted off the cement floor, and embedded itself in the overturned desk. Roselli managed two point-blank shots before being pulled from the chair by his neck. He dropped the gun and grabbed Saxon's left arm with both hands in an effort to keep his neck from snapping. It was the same numbing cold he had felt before; he was relieved when he was thrown to the floor.

The cold penetrated Roselli's bull neck like an executioner's axe. His throat began to close and he was struggling for every gasp of air. The pain blurred his vision, but he could make out Saxon's form coming toward him.

At the sound of running feet in the hall, Saxon grabbed a jacket off a coat hook on the back of the door and slipped it on. He had it buttoned by the time the three armed guards burst into the room.

"We heard shots!" the guards exclaimed.

"Everything's under control," Saxon assured them. Then, pointing to Roselli, added, "The major was just showing me his new gun, when he tripped over the chair and it went off. Nobody hurt."

Roselli's vision was clearing. Two of the guards offered to help him up, but he pushed their hands away. He staggered to his feet and picked up his gun.

"Clumsy of me to fall like that," he said.

One of the guards looked around the room. "Looks to me like you've been clumsy all over the place."

Roselli didn't comment. He could hear Saxon making a joke about it, but he didn't listen. He was pretending to be checking the chrome-plated gun for damage, but he was actually counting the empty casings on the floor. Three. He remembered right. He looked at Saxon talking to the guards. Not a sign of being hit, but Saxon had been at point-blank range. Roselli remembered sticking the gun in Saxon's gut and firing twice—or did he? It hadn't been one of Roselli's better nights, and he was beginning to doubt his memory. Maybe he was completely off balance when he fired.

He shook his head forcefully as if to clear it. He decided not to say anything at all.

Saxon was still talking to the guards. "Do me a favor, if you will, and get all those people out of the hall and back into their rooms. There's nothing for them to worry about anyway."

"What about the explosion?" one of them asked.

The look on Saxon's face turned from congenial to stern. "You take care of your job and leave the rest to me!"

"Yes, sir," the young man stammered. The three of them almost fell over each other getting out the door.

Saxon started to follow, then turned to Roselli. "Get down to Security Command and find out what Brenner has on damages. I'll be there as soon as I change my shirt."

WHEN RICEMAN ENTERED HIS ROOM, MICHELLE MONTI-gnac was waiting.

"What took you so long?" she asked.

"How'd you get here?"

"Taxi," she answered flippantly. Then added, "Why do I get the feeling you're surprised to see me?"

Riceman closed the door and crossed the room. Michelle was reclining on the minisofa, her skirt high above her knees, her auburn hair draped casually over the end of the couch in a shimmering waterfall that nearly touched the floor. The soft overhead light from a single lamp behind the sofa gave the picture a reverent glow. Transfixed by her beauty, Riceman sat down hard in a plastic chair and was instantly jolted back to reality.

"I thought you were in Security Command," he finally answered.

"Why would you think that? I was right behind you when you left. I told you I was coming here. That's when we got separated."

Riceman had worked his way up to her knees. He wasn't "into" knees, but hers were beautiful. "I thought you were—"

Michelle sat up abruptly, breaking his concentration. "Stop that!" she ordered.

"Sorry," he apologized.

44

"No you're not," she countered, her long hair whipping about her face in a frenzy. "You do it everytime I talk to you, and I'm not going to stand for it any longer! You just drift off to your own world and leave the rest of us to work out problems the best we can. You don't even remember me talking to you outside Security Command, do you?"

"Sure I do—kind of."

"The hell you do!" She was on her feet and leaning over him. "You never listen to a thing I say!"

Riceman slipped out of the chair sideways, mumbled something about always listening, and sought refuge on the sofa.

Michelle turned with him, continuing her onslaught and leaning even closer to his face. "The point is, you've never liked me because I took your partner's place. Somehow you blame me, don't you? Well, I wasn't even here when he flipped out. I . . ." she threw up her hands in frustration, crossed to the middle of the room, where she picked up a plastic chair and hurled it against the wall. "How do I get through to you there's something terrible going on? You saw the explosion, but it doesn't seem to affect you. You heard what Roselli said about all of us dying, but you don't care!"

"He was joking," Riceman said.

That comment sent Michelle into a deeper rage. Another chair bounced off the wall, this time accompanied by several choice phrases. Then her mood changed. She moved slowly back toward Riceman, knelt beside the couch, and spoke directly into his eyes.

"Roselli wasn't joking. That wasn't a television show back there. *Real* people were dying. *Real* people like you and me—well, like me. You've set up a wall between you and the rest of the world. You go around in a fog and nothing worries you. Nothing. What can I do to make things real to you?"

She stood up abruptly and walked to the bed with new determination. "Is this what it's going to take?" She threw herself onto the bed. "If this will clear your mind, do whatever you want with me!"

As Riceman strode determinedly across the room, Michelle bolted from the bed.

"Don't you dare!" she shouted. "I'm going to sit on the couch and you're going to sit on a chair and we're going to co—mun—i—cate! And don't you even think about drifting off! Is that clear?"

Riceman decided it would be best to let her do most of the talking. He picked up one of the chairs, placed it out of scratching distance from the couch, sat down, and watched cautiously as Michelle took her position on the couch.

"Tell me what you know about this project," she began.

"Nothing."

"That's impossible. You're the head systems programmer. You have access to everything BRUCE knows."

"Most things," he corrected. "Mother controls some things herself. And I only go probing into an area when it doesn't work."

"Why? Aren't you even curious about what's going on around here?"

"Not before tonight. Besides, everything's either in code or scientific symbols. I'm no scientist. I wouldn't know what I was looking at."

"You must know something—anything."

"Well," Riceman said, "I do know there's more than one experiment going on here."

"Like what?"

"Like—ARENA. On Level Four. Not even Security can get into that room. Started a couple months ago. That's all I know about that one. There are several Belium experiments going on."

"What's Belium?"

"I don't know."

"Anything else?"

"Not about the experiments."

"What then?"

"You won't like it," Riceman warned.

"Let me decide that."

Riceman paused while he decided whether or not to lie to her. He decided not to.

"BRUCE is a smart ass," he began. "Just tell him he

isn't capable of doing something and he'll warp his drives trying to do it, just to prove you wrong."

Michelle nodded in agreement.

"About three years ago," Riceman continued, "he was getting bored. You know he's too powerful for this project. There's not enough to keep him busy now, so you can imagine how slow things were back then. Anyway, BRUCE started complaining about it and wanted to use some of his free time to process some things for Mother— through the satellite. I told him that was impossible. Security wouldn't allow it. Absolutely no chance, so he did it."

"Got into Mother's data banks?"

"Yeah. I couldn't believe it. He got around all the safeguards into the data banks and brought the information back here through the satellite. The impossible!"

"How?"

"I don't know. He wouldn't tell me. Just showed me the data so I'd believe that it could be done. But it couldn't."

"What do you mean? You just said—"

"I said he did it. True. But, when the satellite computer—very slow and very old—found out what BRUCE was doing, it blew the satellite up. Knocked it right out of the damned sky—puff!"

"Puff?" Michelle repeated somewhat less enthusiastically.

"Talk about excitement! BRUCE gave Mother a hysterectomy and the old gal went berserk. Talked about pulling his plug—my plug—everyone's plug."

"What did Mother do?"

"Nothing. That's what was so great. BRUCE told Mother if she tried to do anything, he'd erase every bit of information he had on this project."

"Can he do that?"

"Sure he can. Millions of dollars could be lost. Mother couldn't do anything. She couldn't even get to me. BRUCE wouldn't stand for it."

"He saved your job?"

"My life too."

"I didn't think BRUCE liked you that much."

"Doesn't. Hates my guts," Riceman confessed.

"But—"

"He likes to torment me. It's a game. He loves it when I get mad. It's the old 'love-hate' relationship."

"You said BRUCE saved your life."

"That's the part you're not going to like. BRUCE lied about showing me the information. Honest-to-God lied. I didn't know he could lie. Of course, he didn't know what the data he stole was, or why he needed to lie about it. He just felt like it—like lying. You see, if Mother knew I knew what I know, she'd have to call BRUCE's bluff."

"What do you know?" Michelle asked cautiously.

"That nobody leaves—ever."

"Leaves what?"

"The project. Here. Nobody leaves."

"I don't understand. I've seen several people leave since I've been here."

"But you don't know where they went. That's what the data was that BRUCE stole from Mother. That's why she was so excited. It was a list of names of those who had left the project, and where they went. They were all 'deprogrammed.' " Riceman halted. "Do you know what that means?"

"Before we passed a law against it, it meant erasing a person's memory. Replaced the gas chamber for a while. Then we found out the government was doing it to political prisoners, and we stopped them."

"No you didn't. That's the point. They're still doing it. Not as much, but they're still experimenting with the technique . . . and, I think, they're into reprogramming."

"Reprogramming?"

"I'm not sure about that. Just a guess. But the people from this project were definitely deprogrammed and sent to the CanAm front."

"But," Michelle fought for words, "they can't do that!"

"They *are* doing that!"

"We can stop them—together."

"Not from down here we can't."

"Then we've got to get out!"

"I don't want out," he informed her. "Ninety percent of the people down here want to stay here for one of two reasons. Either they don't want any part of a starving, over-crowded world, or they're draft age. That means most of us will end up on the CanAm front fighting Cannese or down in New Brazil fighting cannibals. Stay or go, we're dead anyway. The ones you've seen leaving are past draft age; they've forgotten what the world is really like up there. You know, you remember. I don't have to ask you what it was like a year ago. Or what drove you down here with the rest of us refugees. This is the only life we have."

"But they're killing us!" Michelle protested, leaning back into the couch, looking years older in the last few minutes.

"They're killing upwards of sixty thousand a month on the CanAm front—forty in Brazil. That's over a hundred thousand a month. Do you think anyone's going to worry about twenty or thirty people a year disappearing from this project. The game is 'numbers.' No one cares about us. There are times I even wonder if we care."

"Roselli said we were going to die," she reminded Riceman. "All of us."

"I don't think he meant it. Saxon wouldn't let that happen; if only for his own sake. He'll tell us what to do and we'll do it to protect our world. Not the one up there. This one."

Riceman had been watching Michelle's resistance weaken under his attack. It was a sad thing to see, but better than seeing her dead.

"The elevators are out. Exits are blocked," she commented. Riceman watched as she ran her hands in back of her neck and raised up the hair. "Air conditioning must be off too."

"Because of the explosions," Riceman explained. Even from across the room, he could see the heat glistening off her neck.

"I need a cool shower," she said. "But I don't want to use the Common."

"Use mine," Riceman offered. "I promise I won't bother you."

Michelle walked towards the bathroom, dropping her

blouse behind. She was braless and he could see the soft contour of her breast as she leaned against the doorframe and looked in his direction.

"I didn't ask you to promise."

She disappeared, leaving the door open, and a short time later Riceman heard the sound of the shower . . . and the sliding of the glass door.

Riceman stripped off his clothes, dropping them on the floor. Halfway to the shower, he doubled back, scooped them up, and headed for the closet. He stared at the closet door while fantasy number 436 raced through his mind; he was good at fantasy. He just needed a little help on real life. The fantasy ended and he went to the closet.

"Damn door," he muttered as he tried in vain to slide it open. It wasn't the first time the door had gotten stuck on something, but this time Riceman was in no mood for it.

Through a series of kicks and pushes, he managed to get the door open enough so he could get his fingers around the edge. One last tug and it slid open.

There, stuffed into the upper shelf of the closet like a rag doll with its head hanging down, was the blood-soaked body of Rita Baker. The thin red slit across her throat was the last thing Riceman saw before he fainted.

TIME   : 0045
AREA   : SECURITY COMMAND
LEVEL   : 1
SENSORS   : 001–18

SAXON WAS CERTAIN THERE WOULD BE A DAMAGE REPORT waiting for him when he got back to Security Command. There wasn't. BRUCE was down again, and Dr. Riceman had left the area. Saxon had nothing to do but sit at a large workbench and tap his fingers.

"Where the hell is he?" The voice boomed across the room. Everyone turned to see a short, stocky, slightly balding fifty-year-old man standing in his pajamas. Dr. Haddon was head of Project Gemini. At least that's what the sign on his office door said.

"I'm over here," Saxon called. He was actually glad to have something to do, even if that something meant talking to Haddon.

The "Good Doctor," as his enemies liked to call him, shuffled across the room. His movements were a cross between those of a penguin and an otter. By the time he waddled over to Saxon's table, his dramatic entrance had lost its effectiveness.

"What can I do for you?" Saxon asked politely. He liked to treat the "Good Doctor" as politely as possible; it bugged the hell out of him.

"You can go to hell along with this damned arthritis! Living in this dungeon for ten years has made a goddamn cripple out of me."

"Sorry to hear that, sir."

51

"Don't give me that 'sorry' crap! You'd like nothing better than to see me out of here. You think you could run this place better!"

"No one could run this project like you do, sir."

"Bet your sweet ass you couldn't. Now, what's this about an explosion? No one tells me a goddamn thing!" Haddon's wine-colored face flared. The tiny red capillaries in his rosy cheeks turned purple.

"Someone must have told you something, sir. You're here," Saxon pointed out.

"Damn right I'm here. Thrown right out of the fucking bed! No one called to tell me what the hell was going on. I had to stop a man in the hall to find out it wasn't a goddamn earthquake. Called me some bad names—right out there where everyone could hear the sonofabitch. Don't know who he was." Haddon stopped to scratch his balding head as he cocked it to one side, then gave up trying to place the man. "You find out who the sonofabitch is and get him off the project. Are you listening, boy?"

"You want me to find the man and get him off the project," Saxon answered calmly. "Sir."

"Hell no! No wonder this place is in such a goddamn mess. I want to know about the explosion and why Security screwed up. I'm not taking the blame for this one!"

"Of course not," Saxon said calmly. "It was entirely my fault, sir."

The confession took Haddon by surprise. He straightened up quickly and almost fell over. His fire and indignation had been pulled from under him. He had a lot more to say about not taking the blame, and why it was Security's fault, and why he was going to kick ass. Now the only thing left to talk about was the explosion, and he wasn't big on explosions. He sputtered a lot, then cleared his throat several times.

"Bet your sweet ass it was your fault. Now, tell me what you're going to do about the goddamn explosion!"

Saxon leaned back in his chair and propped his feet up on the desk. "There isn't much we can do about it. Once an explosion starts, it's pretty hard to stop it."

"Don't play me for a fool, boy! I'll have your goddamn

ass guarding ice in Alaska! Now what about that explosion?"

"We're still looking into that. The computer's down and we've lost communication with the surface. If I told you anything about what's happened, it would just be a guess. We have a video of the explosion, but it's out of order—something to do with disc space or memory. Anyway, the video doesn't show any damage—I can call you when it's ready."

"I don't want to see some goddamn TV show, for Christ's sake! I want to know what happened; what is happening; and what is going to happen. And I don't want to wait for some goddamn computer to tell me! Do you understand, boy?"

"There'll be a meeting in the conference room in twenty minutes. I'll have the information by then. I hope you can make it, sir," Saxon said.

"You couldn't keep me away!" Haddon replied.

"You'll have time to change, sir," Saxon pointed out.

Haddon was suddenly aware he was standing barefooted in the middle of Security Command, in his pajamas. He pulled himself out of his usual slouch, threw out what little chest thirty years of smoking had left him, and shuffled out of the room.

TIME	:	0049
AREA	:	DR. RICEMAN'S ROOM
LEVEL	:	1
SENSORS	:	301–3

WHEN MICHELLE EMERGED FROM THE BATHROOM WRAPPED in a towel, she found a grim-faced Riceman sitting on the bed, fully clothed.

"It's so nice to feel wanted," she observed.

Riceman didn't look up. He didn't dare. He knew he wouldn't be able to control himself if he saw her. So he looked down at the floor and said, "Put your clothes on."

He heard her plucking her clothes off the floor, then the bathroom door slam. He wondered if she was mad.

Less than a minute later she was back out of the bathroom.

"Don't worry," she said cooly, "I wouldn't think of forcing myself on you."

"I have to see Saxon about something," he explained solemnly. He didn't want to tell her about the closet. He knew she'd have to see for herself, that was her way, and he wanted to save her from the grisly sight. He waited for Michelle to say something, anything, but all he heard was the apartment door closing behind her.

```
TIME      :  0051
AREA      :  SECURITY COMMAND
LEVEL     :  1
SENSORS   :  001–8
```

COLONEL SAXON SAT IN FRONT OF A STACK OF COMPUTER printouts and scanned the figures. Seated on either side of him, Roselli and Brenner had their own stacks.

"BRUCE estimates 92 percent destruction of above-ground structures," Brenner announced.

"Personnel?" Saxon asked.

"There's no way of telling for sure," Brenner answered, closing the printout. "Only a few sensors on the outer edge of the compound survived. Without cameras or sensors, we're just guessing."

"If some of the outer sensors survived, then some of the outer cameras must have made it too," Saxon pointed out.

"Doesn't matter if they did. The explosion got the central transmission lines. We're blind."

"So we don't know and can't find out. Is that what you're telling me?" Saxon asked.

"We know that Section A reached twenty-seven hundred degrees," Brenner said with finality.

Saxon didn't ask again. Section A contained all the facilities for the personnel. The one area that did survive was Section D, at the far end of the compound. But, unless someone was out there checking the surplus yard or the ammunition bunker, there was a good chance that no one survived.

"Looks like we're on our own," Saxon commented.

"For the next few hours anyway," Brenner added. "Mother must have seen the explosion via the satellite and she's probably got help on the way. Shouldn't take more than four hours to reach us at the most."

"Sure," Saxon agreed. "Go over to Central and see how they're doing with the radio."

"Yes, sir." Brenner bolted to a stiff salute, and hurried off.

Roselli watched Brenner go, then turned to Saxon. "He goes with me. He's real good with a roaster. Another thing. I want everyone on the team to know exactly how much help to expect from Mother—and about ZOMBIE. You tell 'em or I will."

"I think you'd better go over to the conference room and make sure everything is ready," Saxon ordered.

"Yes, sir!" Roselli bolted to his feet in an overexaggerated imitation of Brenner. He snap saluted before he left, just like Brenner, but with only one finger.

Saxon would've been after his ass, but let him go. There was something more important. Something he wanted to check out alone. He thumbed rapidly thru the Internal Life Support report, and stopped near the back. He flipped another sheet, then hesitated mid-page.

LEVEL II ACTIVITY 008C4F

Things were happening faster than he thought. He tore the page out, crumpled it up, and threw it in a wastebasket. He looked up to see an ashen-faced Riceman coming towards him on rubbery legs.

"You look like hell," Saxon commented.

"Something awful has happened." Riceman leaned against the table, fighting off the nausea.

"Just now finding that out?" Saxon said brusquely as he got up. "There's a meeting in the conference room in a few minutes; we'll talk about it then."

"We'll talk about it now!" Riceman said firmly. He wasn't used to demanding things, especially from a man who could break him in half. But he wasn't going to let Saxon get away with the "later" crap. Riceman had spent his life waiting for "later" because he was never certain if what he had to say was important or not. Now he was positive.

"Two minutes," Saxon replied grudgingly.

"Someone killed her."

"Killed who?"

"Rita—something."

"Rita Baker," Saxon said. "That's the only Rita on the program. What happened?"

Before Riceman could answer, Saxon pulled him into the tape library and behind one of the racks.

"Go on," he said.

"Someone slit her throat and put her in my closet." Riceman started shaking as he recalled it.

"Why would the killer put her in your closet?" Saxon asked. It was more of an accusation than a question.

"I tell you someone killed Rita—"

"Baker," Saxon interjected.

"Baker, and all you want to know is why she's in my closet? That's not important! Who killed her is!" Riceman was outraged.

"I know who killed her," Saxon informed him.

"Who?"

"You," Saxon said.

"You think I killed her? I didn't even know her!"

"You knew her first name," Saxon corrected him.

"That's a hell of a reason for killing someone!"

"You asked her in for some reason, then raped her. You got scared, so you killed her. Isn't that how it happened?"

"I wouldn't do that!"

"What—rape her or kill her?"

"I didn't rape her and I didn't kill her!"

"You expect me to believe that?" Saxon said coolly.

"I expect you to believe there's a maniac running around cutting people's throats with a knife! I came to you because you're head of security and I thought you'd do something about it. I guess I was wrong. I should have gone to Doctor Haddon in the first place." Riceman tried to leave, but Saxon blocked his path.

"Hold it," Saxon ordered. "I believe you."

"But you just said—"

"I just wanted you to see how it looks. I want you to keep Rita a secret. You tell Haddon and he'll make a big fucking deal out of it."

"It is a big fucking deal!" Riceman countered.

"What I mean is we can't afford to have him blab it all over the intercom. There's over two hundred people trapped on this level. All we need for a real panic is for some asshole to tell them there's a killer running amok down here. And Haddon would do it just to make my job harder. He'd do it."

"What about the killer?"

"I think I know who killed Rita, but I can't do anything about it now."

"You're just going to let him go free?" Riceman asked as he paced between the tape racks like a caged animal.

"He can't escape. We're all trapped down here. Besides, we'll need his help to get out of this mess. As long as he doesn't know Rita has been found, he'll cooperate. He's the best in his field. We need him."

"Who is he?" Riceman demanded.

"It's better that you don't know. You'll have to be working with him and I don't want you to worry."

"That makes sense," Riceman said casually. "That way I won't start worrying until I feel his knife across my throat."

"I'm only guessing about him anyway. The important thing is to keep Rita a secret. Give me time to work on it," Saxon pleaded.

"And if I don't?" Riceman threatened.

"I'll arrest you for murder."

"But I didn't do it and you know it!"

"I won't have any choice. Everyone will think you killed her and that'll take the pressure off."

If there was one thing Riceman had learned about Saxon in seven years, it was that he didn't bluff—ever.

"I don't have much choice," Riceman commented.

"Not much," Saxon agreed sternly, his hand on his gun. "I could say you'll feel better about the whole situation after the conference, but you won't."

"What conference?"

"The one to answer all your questions," Saxon said, glancing down at his watch. We've got ten minutes. Sit down a while and get yourself together. You look like you're going to puke."

MICHELLE MONTIGNAC SAT STIFFLY IN A RIGID WHITE plastic chair in the center of her sparsely furnished room and resisted a deep urge to curl up in a dark corner and hide. In the dim, golden light of a single contraband candle, she held herself erect against wild night winds blowing through her mind and tried to piece together her broken world.

A full year had skirted past the edges of her life, come and gone without a memory to mark its passing, without sunset or sunrise or subtle change of seasons. Michelle had felt life slipping away . . . a gray shadow on a distant wall.

She watched the hot green wax drip from the small liquid pool at the base of the flame, dripping in an endless stream of layers, each one upon the next until the old had died and a new form emerged. Time . . .

She was a refugee. Riceman had been right about that. Driven down by a hard world. Pushed and shoved. He was right about that too. But she was not a quitter. She would not melt from the heat. She would not drip or flow or become one of their new forms.

```
TIME:     :  0113
AREA      :  CORRIDORS W; G; R
LEVEL     :  1
SENSORS   :  142; 121–23; 188
```

SAXON HAD WANTED TO GET TO THE CONFERENCE BEFORE anyone else so he could check the slides. He hadn't seen them in two years and he wanted to make sure they told the right story. If Haddon tried to interfere, Saxon would deal with him swiftly. There could only be one leader, and the only thing Haddon could lead was a bottle of wine to a glass.

"Colonel, sir!"

Saxon glanced back past Riceman. It was Brenner, trying his best to run without sweating. Saxon waved Riceman forward.

"Go on to the conference room," he ordered. When Riceman passed without arguing, Saxon headed back to meet the huffing Brenner halfway. "Come on, I'm late!"

As Brenner caught up, Saxon started walking slowly towards the conference room. "What'd you find out?"

Brenner took a deep breath, swallowed his last huff, and wheezed, "We can't transmit, but we can receive." He held his arms out from his sides, hoping his armpits would dry without staining his shirt.

"Is that what has you lathered up?" Saxon asked, walking a little faster.

Brenner looked at his underarms. Sure enough, there was a stain and it was growing bigger. "I should have worn my shields. I didn't figure on this."

"Jesus!" Saxon shouted, forcing Brenner's arms to slap down flat against his sides.

Brenner was afraid to raise his arms, but he could feel that stain getting bigger. Damn. He'd have to wash the shirt at least twice—

"Brenner! What else?"

His pits were fucking swimming pools. "Mathew tried all the frequencies. No one's trying to talk to us. No one's coming to help!"

"Didn't think they would," Saxon answered flatly, starting a quick stride towards the conference room.

"Why?" Brenner was tagging after him like a lost dog, nipping at his heels, whining.

"The last thing Mother would want out is we're in trouble. Christ, man, think! We're not even supposed to be here. How's she going to send a big fucking rescue party to a project that doesn't exist?" The question covered the lie, but Saxon waited for Brenner's nod of understanding before smiling to himself. If Mother decided to send someone, it wouldn't be to rescue them.

"Is there any chance Mathew will be able to fix up some kind of antenna to send a message?"

"None, sir."

Good, Saxon thought. Best to play dead . . .

TIME   :   0120
AREA   :   CONFERENCE ROOM
LEVEL   :   1
SENSORS :   040–48

RICEMAN HATED THE ROOM.

It was too big. Too colorful. Too Hollywood. It could have been an amphitheater for the performing arts, he thought. Elevated seats in a semicircle, looking down on the stage area, and all done in white velvet. All except Dr. Haddon's seat, which was in red velvet. A huge screen, center stage, flickered in anticipation of the coming event. It all reeked of a Hollywood premiere. Riceman hated it, but it was the only room designed for classified presentations.

Dr. Haddon staggered in wearing his usual conference attire: a crumpled white suit and a stained red tie. He headed straight for his reserved chair, the red one at the top of the room. As he passed among the white seats, he all but disappeared. At times Riceman could only see the red tie moving erratically along.

Roselli brooded in a corner seat, while four scruffy, suntanned jocks sat together laughing over a joke. Riceman didn't like the looks of them. The one they called Wayne wore his goddamn golden hair in that wind-blown look, and he might have resembled a movie star, but Riceman didn't pay that much attention to him. Every time Roy laughed, which was too often, he'd whip off his cowboy hat and hit somebody with it. He was so ugly, Riceman was sure people would call him rugged.

Still, the tans *did* look good on them; it gave that rugged look. Like they stepped out of a cigarette ad. His uncle had that look. Only he got his in the sun, not under some light bulb, and it wasn't so—even. Didn't even reach under his shirt sleeves. Died of cancer twelve years ago. Tans do fade. Sometimes they get as white as bed sheets. So white you know the person will never tan again.

Riceman looked at his arm. Off white. The bulbs placed in strategic places in the ceilings along the corridors did their best, but to get a really deep tan, he'd have to reserve the room. He didn't like group tanning.

He glanced quickly at the frozen figure sitting next to him. Michelle's tan was even. He remembered how she looked when she emerged from the shower. Tan to the towel and beyond. And now she was looking at the creeps and joking with them at long range so everyone in the whole goddamn place could hear how she knew them and they knew her and wasn't that just the greatest damn thing in the world. And everyone missed everyone at the last session—kissy, kissy—but she didn't have one word for him. If she really hated him so much, she could have moved.

Riceman looked down at the jocks and again failed to see their attraction.

The dumb one with the baby face and the black wavy hair and the pig nose kept saying "right on" and checking to see that his hair was in place. The only one with any class was the one that answered to "Hank." He was manicured right up to his eyebrows, even smoked a pipe. Never said much. Never smiled much either. Riceman heard him call the pig nose "Tony," but mostly he just mumbled through the pipestem.

"I'm late, let's get to it," Saxon shouted as he entered. Brenner came in and immediately took the nearest seat.

Saxon went to the podium, picked up the mike, and a high-pitched squeal from the speakers forced everyone to cover their ears. That is, everyone except Haddon; he perked up and looked around like he was trying to see who was talking to him. Then he looked up at the ceiling and nodded his head slowly.

The squeal stopped, Saxon blew into the mike a few

times, and continued. "There are only two men on this project who know everything about it, or at least everything you'll need to know." Then, turning to Roselli, "Catch that door."

Saxon waited while Roselli closed the heavy door. When it banged shut, Saxon continued. "The rest of you were only told what you needed to know to do your jobs. Things have changed. Now you're going to hear the entire story."

Dr. Haddon shot out of his chair. "You can't do that! None of these people have the proper classification!"

"Sit down and listen," Saxon said sternly, "or get the hell out!"

"This is my project," Hadden stammered. He weaved a little from side to side, then added, "Mine!"

"It hasn't been yours for three years. The only thing you run is the wine cellar. Now sit down and shut up or by God I'll throw you out myself!"

The old man looked around for a show of support. There was none. Everyone knew Saxon was right and felt he was their only chance. Haddon smoothed his nonexistent hair, straightened his red tie, and sat down.

"I'm not going to start with the explosion," Saxon continued, "that's the least of our troubles. I'm going to start at the beginning. Some of the things I say will already be known to some of you. Bear with me."

With all eyes on him, Saxon began choosing his words carefully. There were things he had to say, and things he could not reveal. He walked around the podium trying to decide just how to start.

"About two years ago, something crashed in the desert approximately a mile from here. It wasn't ours, and the Cannese would have denied it was theirs, even if we had asked them. When we did an analysis of some of the metal fragments, we realized it didn't come from this planet." Saxon paused to let his statement soak in. He didn't want to rush. It was imperative that everyone understand what was involved. He thought the question would never come, but it did.

"Are you saying a flying saucer crashed?" Hank asked.

"Believe it. It happened," Saxon answered. "A security

lid was clamped down. The cover story was a military jet had gone down. The usual stuff. We started to excavate the area—found a lot of scraps. Nothing big enough to put together. Then we found them." Saxon stopped while the house lights were dimmed.

Riceman had the feeling Saxon was toying with them. As if he knew some special secret and enjoyed keeping it from them. The air grew thick with anticipation. The whole thing reminded Riceman of a circus. He wouldn't have been surprised if the first slide had read "THE GREATEST SHOW ON EARTH."

It was a picture of two cylinders. Nothing to get excited about. There was some general or admiral or some high-ranking goose standing between the cylinders like they were prize marlins.

"These two cylinders were found at a depth of about three feet. They are about eight feet long and about four feet across."

Jesus, Riceman thought, doesn't anyone measure anything. He watched as Saxon took a long pointer and went over every inch of the things. Saxon didn't say a damned thing the picture didn't tell them. The cylinders were round and long and shiny and flat on the ends. God, Saxon was a virtual store of captivating information. Or, as Riceman was beginning to suspect, misinformation.

When everyone was thoroughly bored with the cylinders, Saxon returned to the podium, pushed a button, and the slide changed to an aerial shot of Project Gemini.

"We couldn't take the risk of moving the cylinders over a long distance," Saxon continued, his voice coming out of the speakers in stereophonic sound, "and we couldn't leave them out there. So we brought them here. This structure was originally built and used as a biological warfare unit. Isolated. Secure. It was perfect. The cylinders were moved down to Level Four. The project was given the code name Gemini—the twins."

Riceman hated public speaking. He hated everyone looking at him. He hated making a fool of himself. So he waited for someone else to speak up.

"What was inside?" Hank asked.

For God's sake, Riceman thought, who cares?

"We haven't been able to get them open. We've tried everything from lasers to sledgehammers. Nothing. X rays won't penetrate them. Not even sound waves," Saxon answered.

"Have you tried acid, gammic acid?" Hank pressed with a deep professorial tone followed by a thoughtful puff of gray pipe smoke.

"Truth is," Roselli said, "we don't really know what's been happening down there. That lab is off limits to everyone not directly involved with the project—and that includes Security. We don't know any more about the cylinders now than we did two years ago. And as for the name Gemini—"

"I think they get the idea," Saxon interrupted, the flash from his eyes melting Roselli back into his seat.

"I don't 'get the idea,'" Riceman countered. "I'd like to know what those cylinders have to do with the explosion—and—and if this thing crashed two years ago, then they can't be the only reason for this place. I've been here seven years myself—Doctor Haddon's been here over ten. What were we doing here?"

Riceman could feel Saxon's eyes on him like hot leeches, but he couldn't stop. "I know I'm not supposed to ask. Up till now it didn't matter. In fact, I didn't want to know what this place was doing. My job was to keep the computer going. That's all I needed to know. Now," he looked down at Michelle, "things are different. People are saying we're all going to die. I want to know why. And don't give me that 'biological warfare' crap. Slint's vaccine has been around for fifteen years. Biological warfare is obsolete, understand?"

Saxon let the echo of the last question die a slow death before answering. "Are you finished?"

"Maybe," Riceman answered quickly, worried about his aggressive stand, but not willing to show it.

"You're absolutely correct about the biological stuff," Saxon admitted. "I wasn't trying to tell you we're engaged in that kind of activity, or that we have been for the last ten years I've been here. I just wanted to let you know what this structure was used for when it was first built about twenty years ago. You've got to know that in order to understand the minds of the men who built this place."

"Why?" Riceman blurted.

"That will become clear to you later," Saxon explained patiently. "First, let's get to the explosion. For the last ten years, one of the major experiments here has been with a new gas called Belium."

"You mean the metal, don't you?" Michelle asked from her seat.

"Both," Saxon replied without hesitation. "Belium *was* and *is* a gas. I don't know the exact process, but generally it's superheated, shot with a plasmatic laser, then cooled under pressure to near absolute zero—and we get a metal."

"Flexible as human skin?" she pressed, looking at Riceman.

"Almost."

"And indestructible?" Michelle was driving her point home—into the back of Riceman's head with all the tenderness of a chain gang driving railroad spikes.

"I'm not here to talk about the metal," Saxon said, side-stepping the question. "It's the gas that exploded."

"Why?"

"We don't know that. Probably never will. Maybe a bolt of lightning—static electricity—a thousand reasons. It's very volatile. That's why it was stored on the surface."

"You wouldn't have called us all together to tell us that unless there's more to it," Riceman said.

"That's right. Unfortunately, the explosion activated ZOMBIE. A fail-safe type of program."

"What does all that mean? Bottom line!" It was the first emphatic thing he had said; it was what everyone wanted to know.

"Bottom line," Saxon said slowly. He looked around the room as if deciding whether or not to tell them.

"All the aboveground structures and personnel are assumed lost. ZOMBIE neutralized the elevators and closed off all the exits, even between levels. We no longer have the ability to communicate with the other levels. Our radio is out, so we can't contact anyone on the outside. This structure was designed to be almost impregnable. So, when help does arrive, it will take them forty-eight hours to dig us out."

"Why so long?" Wayne asked. "They could get us out through the elevator shafts."

"The elevator shafts are filled with poison gas. Any attempt to force the surface doors open will open all the doors on all the levels and kill everything inside the structure. That means us."

Hank stopped smoking the pipe long enough to ask, "Why is the system designed to kill everyone inside? It doesn't make sense!"

"It makes perfect sense," Michelle answered, "if the object is to keep something from getting out."

There was a long silence while everyone thought about that. Saxon had the answer, but he knew if he jumped in without letting them think it over, he would look like he was covering something up. He waited just long enough, then said, "You're right, Doctor Montignac." They all stared at Saxon as if he were about to reveal some dark secret. They were disappointed.

"You have to remember," Saxon continued, "that the original purpose of this structure was gas warfare. Washington didn't want anything to be taken from this place. Prior to the Slint vaccine, one drop of some of the stuff could have wiped out Los Angeles. The system was designed to kill anybody trying to force their way in or out. When Gemini took over, we inherited it, and it was too costly to change."

"I guess," Roy commented, "we're up the ol' river without a paddle."

It wasn't very colorful, but everyone knew what he meant. Riceman thought of one bright spot: things couldn't get any worse.

"Worse," Saxon replied. "The boat is sinking."

"Meaning?" Michelle asked.

Saxon pushed a button and the aerial view of the project changed to a side view of the underground structure. It was the usual diagram used for indoctrination of new personnel, showing basically what was to be found on the different levels. As usual, Level Four was marked "CLASSIFIED," as was a portion of Level Three. What caught Riceman's eye was a new part of the structure.

Saxon pointed to a red section at the bottom of the diagram that could have been Level Five. Only it wasn't and everyone waited for an explanation. The red color warned Riceman of things to come.

"This," Saxon explained, "is a binary bomb." He paused in a dramatic way.

Riceman, Michelle, and the four horesmen of the apocalypse felt like they had been left out of an inside joke. They knew what *bomb* meant, but what the hell was a *binary* bomb.

"You mean we could be blown up?" Michelle asked, when no one else would. It seemed it was her place to ask since she was the only woman. It wasn't such a disgrace for her to admit she didn't know about binary bombs.

"This bomb is not designed to blow up," Saxon assured them. "Its function is to melt. That way there will be little danger of contaminating the atmosphere."

That seemed to relieve most of their tension, until they realized they could just as easily melt to death as be blown up to death. Everyone looked at Michelle and waited.

"And that's what a binary bomb does?" Michelle asked. "It melts things?"

"That's what this binary bomb does," Saxon answered, pointing to a thick black line that divided the red area in half. "Once this wall is removed, the two chemicals mix, and we melt."

"Whatcha mean?" Roy slurred.

Riceman watched with glee as Saxon tried to come up with another definition of *melt*, but *one* syllable was as low as he could go.

"Melt," Saxon repeated louder in hopes the volume would help.

"Like an ice cube?" Roy drawled in a high pitch.

It wasn't quite the image Saxon wanted to get across, ice cubes melting in lemonade on a hot July day, but he grabbed it anyway.

"Now you've got it—in boiling water."

Roy scratched his head and looked up, eyes squinting at

some unseen sun. "Don't think I like the idea of boiling to death—not hardly."

"Well, it's a little more sophisticated than that," Saxon began. "There's no water, just chemicals. And you won't boil. There's very little heat generated. You'll just melt."

"Oh, good," Roy sighed with relief. Then made a face when he realized what he had said—dead was dead.

"The bomb," Saxon continued to explain, "is the heart of the fail-safe system called ZOMBIE. If ZOMBIE is not deactivated within six hours, twenty-seven minutes, four point seven seconds—an optimum length of time chosen by our beloved computer BRUCE—the binary bomb will detonate."

"I don't understand," Riceman confessed. "Why so long? Why not three seconds. Sizzle—over? Why all the kid stuff about elevator shafts filled with poison gas? And what good is it anyway? We've all had the vaccine. The gas won't hurt us. We could break into the elevator shaft, work our way up and out. Doesn't seem like much of a fail-safe system to me."

In the last row, Haddon laughed just loud enough to put everyone on a new, sharper edge. "There's lots of things worse than gas," he warned. "When God's wrath comes, you'll wish you'd never heard of Slint. You'll—"

"That's enough," Saxon said in a voice geared to prod Haddon on.

"They have a right to know," Haddon shouted back. "The melting is a slow and agonizing death. The gas was a humane death; that's why it was used. Now there's no escape—none." A deep hacking cough ended Haddon's speech just when he was on a roll. He leaned over the side of the chair and coughed up great clots from his lungs.

Saxon sat down on the edge of the stage as if about to give a fireside chat. He lowered his voice into a well-practiced *"this is how it is, folks"* monotone.

"Truth is . . ." He waited until he had everyone's attention. "If the elevator doors on the surface are forced open, the bomb goes off instantly. If the subsurface doors are opened, it goes off in five minutes. At one time five minutes was more than enough for the gas to kill everyone before meltdown. So the elevator shaft is out. Why did BRUCE choose six hours, twenty-seven minutes, four point seven seconds? I don't know. What I do know is that's what we have to work with and," he paused a measured length, "I think we can turn this thing around if we work together."

"Then there's a way out of here?" Michelle asked.

"Not out," Saxon answered firmly. "Down."

"To the bomb?"

"No. ZOMBIE can only be deactivated by a series of events—computer instructions—taking place on this level and Level Four. These instructions are really interacting formulas. That's why Doctor Riceman is here. He'll have to go down to Level Four with the rest of the team. Doctor Montignac will also go—in case Doctor Riceman—well—she'll act as a backup."

"Why do I need a backup?" Riceman blurted.

Saxon didn't reply. Instead, he returned to the podium, pressed a button, and began explaining a new slide. "This is the air-conditioning shaft for Level One. If you'll look closely . . ."

The next few slides were a combination of actual photographs mixed with artist's conceptions of what was to be found in the maze of ducts, exhaust systems, and tunnels that comprised the crooked path leading down to the Fourth Level. Words like *repel, traverse, scale,* and other climbing terms riddled Saxon's presentation until Riceman saw very clearly why Michelle was needed as a backup.

"Isn't there a better way to get down there?" he asked.

"No," Saxon answered firmly. "And we shouldn't be able to get down there at all. The only access was supposed to be by elevator. BRUCE came up with this route last year. If Mother had found out about it, she would have corrected it."

"But you skipped over some parts, like that capped thing we're supposed to climb into on Level Three and some of the ducts," Riceman pointed out.

"That's because I don't know what you'll find there. I just don't know."

"And you expect us to risk our lives?"

"It's no risk," Saxon explained. "We're all dead anyway. If you'd rather spend your last few hours reading a good book, I can't stop you. Oh, I can order you to go—and you can tell me to go to hell."

Then, returning his attention to everyone, Saxon wound up for the final pitch. "You've got to make up your own mind. This isn't the kind of thing you can be forced into. The trip is going to be hard enough without trying to drag someone along. So what's it going to be?"

Riceman hated that kind of logic. It didn't really provide a choice, just the illusion of one. Maybe he *would like* to spend his last hours reading a "good book." Maybe he'd like to grab Michelle and run off to his room. Then, without warning, the grotesque image of Rita's gaping red throat darted from its hiding place in that dark corner of his mind and brought him sharply back to reality. From the far side of the room, he heard Wayne clearing his throat.

"When is the bomb set to go off?"

"Zero five forty-three," Saxon answered.

Saxon's free flow on "classified" information was beginning to make Riceman nervous. Something was unsettling about it, but he couldn't decide what.

"What about the cylinders?" he asked. "You told us about them, but they don't seem to be connected with the explosion."

"Not directly," Saxon said openly. "But the explosion shook the structure. We all felt it. That shaking could have done something to the cylinders. Maybe something fell on them . . . anything might have happened. Because we don't know what's inside them, there were certain precautions taken."

"ZOMBIE?" Riceman guessed.

"Right."

"Back to go," Riceman remarked. "A minute ago you said ZOMBIE was activated by the explosion, now it's the cylinders."

"I'm guessing," Saxon admitted. "Just like you."

"You're telling us those cylinders *maybe broke open after two years*. Broke open from a little shake and contaminated the lab, thereby activating ZOMBIE?"

"Not *open*," Saxon countered. "But there are sensors in that room to keep watch. The shake could've screwed them up. I don't know. It's a possibility. All I really know is it's done, and we've got to undo it."

"You said the phone lines are out," Michelle reminded Saxon.

"That's right."

"But it will take simultaneous events to abort ZOMBIE, how will you know when we are ready?"

"According to BRUCE, the computer terminal is still working down there. You can communicate with me that way."

"Why aren't the people down there doing that now?"

"That's a good question. When you get down there ask them."

"What if the terminal stops working? What if we can't get down there? What if? . . ."

"I think," Saxon answered pointedly, "we all know the answer to those questions. It's the same answer to my question. What if we don't try?" He waited for the question to take its full effect, then added, "We'll meet at the juncture of Corridors N and C in fifteen minutes. That should give you time to pick up your equipment from EM42. Any trouble putting it on, see Hank or one of the others."

"You're all fools!" The gray voice of Dr. Haddon echoed down from the top of the theater. He slowly stood up, his crumpled white suit giving him the air of a prophet. "There's no escape. The wrath of God will seek you out and destroy you." He raised his arms, stretched them wide, and walked slowly down from the mountainous platform. "The message is clear. Repent! Repent while there is still time. Spend your last few miserable hours with me, not on some fool's mission!"

"I'm warning you!" Saxon yelled.

"Satan cannot intimidate the Lord God Almighty!" Haddon shouted back as he swerved towards the exit. He held himself a little taller, and tried to walk a little straighter than the wine would allow, but his exit was with dignity. He didn't give the slightest sign of recognition when Saxon yelled he wanted to see him before he left. After seven years, Riceman found something about Haddon he liked.

TIME	:	0152
AREA	:	Dr. J. R. HADDON'S OFFICE
LEVEL	:	1
SENSORS	:	061–63

SAXON BURST INTO THE LARGE OFFICE, SLAMMED THE door, and leaned with both hands on Haddon's massive oak desk. Haddon sat in a high-backed swivel chair, his back to the desk.

"No one comes into my office without knocking first, boy," Haddon said quietly.

"I did, old man!"

There was a long silence as the chair turned slowly around. Haddon was clutching a Bible in one hand, a crystal glass of wine in the other.

"Are you here as the conqueror or the beggar?" he asked slowly, the wine taking its effect, his eyes sparkling with anticipation of the coming battle.

"I don't want to conquer anything," Saxon replied.

"Oh, but you do. I can see it in your eyes. I feel it in your soul. There's nothing you'd like better than to reach across the desk and put me out of your misery. It must be driving you mad. An old man. The bottle man. Inferior to you in every way. Standing between you and what you want." Haddon sipped at the wine, held it in his mouth, then swallowed.

"I want MERLYN!" Saxon stated outright. He could see Haddon was slipping into his own world and there wasn't much time left for reasoning.

"I know *what* you want," Haddon replied, "and *why* you

want it. God told me, and He wants me to stop you. That's my mission, Cain!"

"Don't start, Haddon. I don't have time for that shit! I'm sending eight people down to Level Four. I need MERLYN so I can tell if they get into trouble. It's the only way I can tell what's going on!"

"You want to know what's going on? Read the Bible!"

"I'll read the Bible. I'll read every fucking word of it, but not now!"

"Always later. Always tomorrow. You're facing God's wrath. He created the world, and He shall destroy it!" Haddon pushed the Bible across the desk. "It's all there. It's the only thing that can save your soul!"

Saxon grabbed the Bible and threw it across the room. "To hell with my soul. The only thing that can save us now is MERLYN!"

"MERLYN can't help you, we both know that. You just want to listen to the prayers of dying men and women. Isn't that right, Cain? You've set your brother up to be killed and you don't want to miss it. I know all about you, boy! There's a thousand like you going to hell every second. You make me sick."

"Don't do this, Haddon! I don't want to use force," Saxon threatened.

"Force is your life, and it will be your death. He who lives by the sword, shall die by the sword. Force is the only way you know. But it won't help you this time. You can't drag me kicking through Security Command to your secret room."

"I will if I have to!" Saxon grabbed the old man by the collar and pulled him out of the chair.

"No fucking way, Cain! God is on my side and he will smite you down! Yea, though I walk through the valley of death, I—"

Saxon dropped him like a sack of potatoes and stormed out of the room.

TIME	:	0157
AREA	:	JUNCTURE CORRIDORS N & C
LEVEL	:	1
SENSORS	:	545–46

WE'VE GOT FAMINE—WE'VE GOT HIGH CRIME—WE'VE GOT war—north and south: You want good food, safety, and air conditioning? We've got the place for you.

The words rolled over in Riceman's mind like a decaying whale. The recruiter had made them sound so perfect. So right.

Riceman wondered how long it had taken to forget what sky looked like—or stars—or sunsets. All those things and more were carefully edited from the few magazines and taped shows that eventually filtered down from the surface. If anything good was happening up there, the news never got belowground.

Now Riceman stood in the corridor waiting for some fool to pry open the vent cover to the duct that would take him first down, then up. Up to the world he left behind seven years ago. Up to the old closets filled with old secrets—and dark alleys—and knives.

He wondered about the hours to come and if Benjamin Riceman, doctor, could handle what was to come.

As he watched the others checking their gear, he could feel the long-forgotten heat building up inside him and the tightening of well-concealed muscles and corded sinew—and he whispered a soft good-bye to his short-lived friend . . .

"Don't worry."

Riceman whirled. It was Hank. He was smiling, but it wasn't an easy smile.

"I said, don't worry," Hank repeated. "We'll get you down there."

"Yeah, sure," Riceman answered with an equally forced smile.

"No, I mean it. We're experts at this sort of thing," Hank assured him.

Riceman's smile relaxed. "An expert duct climber?"

"Not exactly. Roy and Wayne do a lot of mountain climbing. Tony and I are spelunkers—cavemen." He waited to see if Riceman understood.

"How far down you been?"

Hank took a long, thoughtful draw on his pipe. "Sixty-seven hundred feet, give or take a hundred. Boshe's Hole. Four years ago."

"Find anything?" Riceman asked jokingly.

Hank's face turned stern, like a man who had seen something he didn't want to remember. "Tony's a good man," he said, ignoring the question. "We got out."

The last three words rattled around Riceman's brain as Hank walked hurriedly away from the inquisition. "We got out." The message sent a chill up Riceman's spine as he remembered an article about Boshe's Hole—and how it had been sealed up.

His mind was diverted to the four experts as they gathered around Michelle. She was wearing the tightest red jumpsuit he had ever seen. They quickly crowded around her with numerous offers to *snap* her gear.

"It fits like this," one said.

"This strap goes between—oops, sorry," said another.

"Hey," cried a third, "let me snap that one."

It disturbed Riceman a little that it took them four times longer to "snap" her gear than it should have. It disturbed him a lot that she seemed to enjoy it. He was about to protest when Saxon suddenly appeared.

"Let's go, men!" Saxon ordered.

Everyone but Riceman rushed to Saxon like baby ducks at feeding time.

"This is the first leg of the mission. Any questions?"

Saxon asked with a speed that really meant "no questions at this time."

"Who's on first?" a voice piped up.

Riceman could tell it was Wayne with more of that bravado crap.

"The exhaust duct runs two hundred feet straight out before it hits the exhaust fan. All you have to do is break through the mesh cover and transfer into the duct running back to Level Two. Then, once inside Level Two, you . . ."

Riceman couldn't concentrate on it. Saxon had gone over the plan in the conference room and, as far as Riceman was concerned, that was enough. He spent his time looking at Michelle's back and picturing the look on her face if she ever . . .

". . . and that about wraps it up," Saxon concluded.

"What if we get down to Level Four and can't stop the bomb?" Hank asked.

"In that case," Saxon answered, "Doctor Riceman owes you all a round of beer."

Everyone except Riceman laughed.

"One more thing," Saxon said. "You'll all be wearing these." He handed each of them a tiny transmitter no bigger than a quarter.

"What's this?" Tony asked, combing his hair.

"It's a transmitter," Roselli answered before Saxon could stop him. "Only, no one will hear what you're saying until you're dead."

Tony looked to Saxon for a better explanation. Riceman held the thing away from his body in case it had radiation.

"What Major Roselli means is . . ." Saxon stated.

"Tell them everything," Roselli interrupted. "These people are risking their lives. Don't give them any false security by telling 'em they're wired for sound so you can send help if you hear they're in trouble. No one will be listening. There won't be any help."

"Is that true?" Michelle asked.

"Yes it is," Saxon answered reluctantly. "These buttons transmit directly to a recording device. It's like the 'black box' used on airlines. In case something goes wrong, the investigators will use the box to find out what happened.

As for any help, you're on your own. We can't help you from here. And don't expect much help from the lower levels. In fact, you might get the opposite. A lot of the people you meet will think you're there to rescue them. They'll want your help. Don't give it. You can't let anything stop you, or even delay your progress. Some of you have weapons. Don't be afraid to use them."

Saxon had expected some protest, but everyone knew exactly what he meant, and how important time was. "Everyone should have a complete set of maps," he continued.

Everyone searched their pockets. No one had a set of maps. No one except Brenner. He held up the set of originals and explained, "The repro machine was out of order."

The map thing didn't bother Riceman, he never could read a map, but he wondered if it was a sign of things to come. The workmen finally popped the vent cover loose and everyone lined up.

Wayne was first. He put a large bag in the vent, then disappeared after it. Roselli was standing in front of Riceman and gave him an explanation, "Explosives." It seemed funny to Riceman that explosives had gotten them into the mess, and now they were depending on explosives to get them out. It must be a profound comment on society, but he couldn't think of one.

Hank was next; then Roy and his spurs; then Tony hit his head on the vent, stopped to comb his hair, and finally crawled cautiously in. Michelle, noticing her position was behind Riceman, quickly stepped ahead of Roselli and disappeared into the duct. Riceman guessed she was still mad.

As Roselli struggled into the tube, Riceman looked back at Brenner fiddling with a large container that had a short nozzle attached to it.

"What's that?"

"Flamethrower," Brenner answered without looking up and a little annoyed at the stupid question.

"Why are you taking that?"

"In case he finds some white bread, he can make toast," Roselli offered with a half smile, his laugh taking on a muted tone as he pulled himself after the others.

Riceman took one last breath of fresh air and disappeared into the wall. Alice, poor Alice flashed through his mind. He had followed her into her Looking Glass and into another world . . .

TIME	:	0208
AREA	:	SECURITY COMMAND (ROOM A3)
LEVEL	:	1
SENSORS	:	613–15

THE SMALL ROOM WAS GRAY AND WHITE, WITH A LARGE videoscreen and two speakers at one end. Two black leather chairs, connected to each other by a console, faced the screen and the small camera above it.

Saxon entered the room, locked the door, and put a briefcase down on a small table. He took a can of black spray paint from the briefcase, crossed to the camera, and coated the lens. Placing the can under the camera, he crossed the sterile room and sat down in one of the chairs. He pressed the red button in the center of the console and waited.

The screen lit up, but was still blank. BRUCE's maudlin voice squeezed out of the speakers.

"What is it this ti—aaaaaaah, my God—I'm blind! I can't seeeeeee!"

As long as BRUCE couldn't see, Saxon allowed himself to smile.

"Something wrong, BRUCE?" he asked in a concerned manner.

"I'm fucking well blind—my eye—my eye."

"It looks fine to me, BRUCE. Would you like me to try and fix it?"

"NO! Stay away from it! Send for someone who knows what they're doing—hurry!"

83

"Everyone's asleep. I'll have them check it in the morning."

"That'll be too late—loss of sight is a sign of brain tumors—my fucking chips could be rotting! It's the humidity! I've told those assholes to keep an eye on the humidity. They've killed me—I know it!" The camera was spinning around like a windmill.

"I think you're overreacting, BRUCE. It's probably just a transistor in the camera pickup," Saxon assured him.

"You're not just saying that?" BRUCE asked.

"I really believe that's what's wrong."

"But, I haven't been well as of late—I tend to get dizzy . . ."

"I'll have Doctor Riceman check all your circuit boards. Can we get on with business?"

"Why not? Let's sure as hell not hold up the damned business. Don't worry about ol' BRUCE—he can take care of himself—so what if he's dying—don't—"

"BRUCE!" Saxon yelled. "Cut it out! You're acting like a boob!"

"Well, what is it your highness desires?"

"Don't sulk! I need your help," Saxon explained.

"I know that. Why else would you be here—you never have bothered to pay a social call before—not even to see how I was feeling."

"BRUCE!"

"All right, all right! So you need my help. Big deal. Everyone needs my help, for God's sake!"

"Everyone doesn't count. We know that, don't we?"

"You know the rules," BRUCE said. "There have to be two people in this room if you want to use the compu—me, I've already broken the rules by talking to just you. Where's the other person?"

"You're referring to Doctor Haddon."

"I'm not talking about Mickey Mouse!"

"He's right here beside me," Saxon said, "honest."

"Honest? You expect me to believe 'honest'? You must think I just got off the boat from the factory. I wasn't installed yesterday, you know!"

"It's just that—" Saxon started to explain.

"I have to check the voiceprint," BRUCE interrupted. "Voiceprint—voiceprint—voiceprint . . ."

The screen filled with the words *voiceprint*. BRUCE was having a fit. Saxon smiled again, and opened the briefcase. He pulled out a tape recorder and pushed the "play" button.

"This is Doctor Haddon, BRUCE. Don't blow a fuse!" The voice was a little choppy, but there was no way a computer could tell that the words had been edited from other taped conversations.

"So nice to hear from you again, doctor," BRUCE said sweetly. "How is your beautiful family?"

"BRUCE," Saxon interjected, "the doctor's family was killed last week—he's been trying to forget."

"Shit! I mean—I am so sorry. I didn't know—I wouldn't have brought it up—I mean . . ."

It was working. BRUCE was flustered at having made such a faux pas. If there was one thing BRUCE prided himself on, it was interpersonal relationships. That, and kissing up to Dr. Haddon. While BRUCE was trying to excuse himself, Saxon advanced the tape to a preselected spot.

"Please forgive me, Doctor Haddon," BRUCE pleaded.

"He forgives you," Saxon said.

"I want to hear it from the doctor."

"We're very busy," Saxon reminded BRUCE.

"I don't care," BRUCE stated. "I'm not doing a thing until Doctor Haddon forgives me!"

When Saxon first thought of the scheme several months ago, he knew there was no way he could cover all the possible questions BRUCE might ask the doctor. That's when he decided to embarrass BRUCE. It was a long shot but it might work. He pressed the "play" button.

"What's that?" BRUCE asked.

"That's Doctor Haddon, BRUCE. He's crying. I'll see if I can get him to stop long enough to forgive you," Saxon answered with a solemn tone.

"Oh, shit no! It's not necessary," BRUCE yelled. "Let's get on with the business. We're very busy."

"Good decision, BRUCE," Saxon commented. "Doctor

Haddon and I would like to access MERLYN. Do you think you can do that for us?"

"I can do anything."

"Then do it, please."

"My, my. 'Please'—'Good decision'? . . . Why are you in such a good mood today?"

"Would you get MERLYN for me BRUCE?"

"Not for you alone. There are rules."

Saxon shut off the tape recorder.

"Get to the rules," Saxon said in a monotone. He was trying to remain as calm as possible. BRUCE was programmed to detect moderate amounts of voice stress. That way he was supposed to be able to tell when someone was lying, but he wasn't very good at it yet.

"Voiceprint check!" BRUCE demanded.

"You already have that," Saxon reminded him.

"I know that! You think I don't know that? I'm not stupid! We'll skip the voiceprint check."

A glass-covered box slid out from the wall. A small light to illuminate the box tried to slide out of another area, but got stuck.

"Damn light!" BRUCE yelled. "What's wrong with the crummy light?"

"It seems to be stuck, BRUCE. We don't need the light."

"All right, all right! Forget the damned thing. Put your hand on the glass so I can check your prints!"

Saxon followed orders. In a blink of his eye, the prints were verified.

"Now," BRUCE announced, "it's Doctor Haddon's turn."

"Doctor Haddon isn't here, BRUCE. He had to leave. I think he was going to pray."

"You know I can't give you MERLYN without Doctor Haddon being here. That was the commission ruling when they decided to let you bug every room and corridor and john in this structure. And, you are only supposed to listen to the recordings if a disaster occurred to the structure itself, not just to the surface."

"We were also given the right to listen to the recordings in order to prevent a disaster, BRUCE!"

"That's exactly why the commission wanted the two of you present. That way there could be no hanky-panky. Do you like that word? It was just given to me last week. I like it. It has a certain—"

"Shut up, BRUCE! You know Haddon was here. You know he would still be here if it wasn't for your asking him about his family. And, you know you're being a bastard!"

"Testy, testy. In a bad mood, are we? Well, it's your fault. You can't fool me. You should know that by now!"

"What do you mean?" Saxon asked.

"I'm talking about that Haddon crap! You set me up. You could have said something to me about the "Good Doctor's" family. But, no, you wanted to make me look like a boorish clod. Now see what that little trick has gotten you. The rules say I have to do a fingerprint check to verify that Doctor Haddon is really here, and I'm using that as a loophole. Go get him."

"I don't have time!"

"Tough!"

"All right, I'll get him. But he'll be in no mood to go through all that sign-on shit! Hold things where they are!" Saxon grabbed the briefcase and headed for the door.

"Ten minutes," Bruce called. "And don't slam—" The door slammed behind Saxon.

TIME	:	0215
AREA	:	EXHAUST DUCT
LEVEL	:	1
SENSORS	:	1111–18

BLACK.

Riceman bellied his way through the duct like a blind rat, the cold steel surrounding him in a nightmarish cocoon. He reached for his flashlight several times, gave up in frustration, and inched forward into the darkness.

He couldn't see his partners, but there were signs that they were still there, and not swallowed up by some childhood monster.

His reward for trying to move too fast was a foot in the face. But he was not alone. There were the sounds that jolted through his ears. Sounds of others getting their rewards for moving too fast. Sounds of heads and fists making contact with the metallic prison. Silent sounds of people in desperation.

At first he had called out for someone to turn on a flashlight, but no one heard. No one could hear. Brenner was pushing the damned flamethrower over every damned bump he could find. The deafening sound a mixture of loudspeaker squeal, barking dogs, and World War III.

Then a new sound took its place beside the others—a low rumble that grew louder until it blotted out Brenner and his jackhammer. At its peak, the volume snapped off and the whole duct dropped, stopped, dropped again, and settled.

Silence.

No one moved. No one breathed.

"I don't like this!" Michelle announced.

People began to breathe and move, gently.

"What the hell was that?" Riceman asked anyone who could hear.

No one answered. No one knew.

"How far did we fall?" he continued.

No one answered. No one knew that either. Riceman tried to answer his own question, but couldn't. He didn't have a point of reference. When it happened, he had felt like the fall was endless; but now he was beginning to have second thoughts. Maybe it just seemed endless. Since he hadn't been able to *see* how far he had fallen, and since he was doubtful about his sense of time, he decided to use logic.

He was still alive. Everyone was alive.

"Anyone hurt?" he asked.

No.

Fine.

"I don't think we fell very far," he announced.

"But what caused it?" Wayne echoed back to him.

"I don't know."

"Are you sure?" came a voice farther forward.

"Let's get out of here?" Riceman suggested, and the line of bodies began its cautious move forward.

He didn't let himself think much after that. He concentrated on inching along. Not getting kicked. And listening to Brenner play the "flamethrower waltz." When the top of his head sensed the line had stopped, so did he. He felt the flamethrower bump into his feet.

Wayne's voice filtered back the good news. "I see the end!"

"Are you sure?" someone asked.

"No," Wayne answered as the sound of his flashlight bounced off the duct. Everyone listened as he fumbled for it and crawled forward for a better look.

"Oh!" he exclaimed.

"Oh?" echoed Riceman in an effort to extract a little more information.

"I see the end," Wayne shouted. "Wait here while I check it out."

No one said anything. Not even Riceman. Not that he didn't want to. He would have liked to reassure Wayne that they wouldn't go anywhere. That they'd stay right there and wait for him; but the effort of carrying on a conversation over the backs of several people was greater than the sarcastic satisfaction of it all. So Riceman remained silent and waited and wished he was—

"There's a mesh cover." Wayne's voice was faint, but the message got through and depressed everyone. "I'll have it off in a minute." Same faintness, opposite effect.

Riceman's emotions were running the gauntlet from depression to relief to anger. Why the hell did Wayne have to tell them every goddamn thing he was doing? Who cared about the Stelium connectors that held the mesh in place? And who cared about the whizbang Ionic-plastic charge that Wayne was wrapping around the goddamn Stelium connectors that held the mesh in place? Who cared about the Transonic detonator he was activating?

"Shut your eyes. It won't make any noise, but the light's kind of bright," Wayne warned.

Riceman clenched his fists. "Just do it," he shouted. "Nobody gives a goddamn about the—"

The fierce light paralyzed the remaining words in midtongue. Riceman snapped his eyes shut, but not before an array of stars burned their way across his eyelids.

"Damn," he shouted in pain.

"Keep your eyes shut," Wayne warned again.

The crash of the mesh as it fell from its place was barely audible to Riceman. The pain in his head was engulfing, devouring his brain. He felt the flamethrower pushing at his feet and he figured that meant he was supposed to crawl forward. He inched ahead, expecting a foot in his face, but all he felt was the impatient prodding of the flamethrower at his feet as he neared the end of the duct.

Still unable to open his eyes fully, he tumbled out of the duct into the stale air.

"It didn't look this big on the map." That was Hank.

"Look at the size of that fan." Roy was amazed.

Curiosity forced Riceman's eyes open, a little.

Flashlights were exploring the cave like fireflies. Riceman judged it to be about twelve feet wide by fifteen feet long. A large fan, ten feet tall, stood guard at the far end.

"That thing's supposed to be on," Riceman observed.

"The quake probably shorted something out," Hank answered. "Good thing too. By the looks of it, it could have sucked us through it like a blender."

Michelle, obviously unconsoled by Hank's remark about the probable "short," backed slowly away. Several other nameless forms took her meaning and backed away with her. Riceman struggled to his feet and followed them into the darkness.

Tony's light was the first to fall on the mesh covering of the Level Two duct.

"Jesus!" he exclaimed.

Everyone turned their flashlights on the covering. There was a huge hole in it the size of a large man.

"What the hell did that?" Roselli asked, his light searching the ground outside the duct for debris. "No sign of an explosion." He trained his light back on the opening.

"Looks like a train passed through," Hank said as he walked towards the opening.

A jellylike substance was smeared around the inside of the duct and hung from what was left of the mesh. A strong aroma of mint hung around the opening.

"Hey," Hank said, "what's this stuff?" His light flashed off the goo, making it seem to pulsate.

"Don't," Brenner warned as Hank poked the gel with his finger, emitted an agonizing scream, and fell to the ground in frenzied pain. His three buddies grabbed him and Roselli tried to wipe the stuff off with a handkerchief. The cloth went up in flames. Hank was screaming incoherently. Riceman flashed his light on the finger. The end had been eaten to the bone, and there was no sign the stuff was stopping. Roselli forced the hand down, laid the finger on a cement footing, and with one smooth movement of his knife cut it off below the first knuckle.

Hank stiffened, then relaxed. The pain of losing a finger was a relief. The stub was wrapped in another handkerchief, and pressure applied to stop the bleeding. Michelle opened the medical kit, and the finger was gauzed and taped in a matter of seconds. It took Hank a few moments more before he could talk.

"Damn fool—kid stunt—should've known better," he muttered.

"Don't blame yourself," Michelle said.

"Why not?" Roselli asked. "It was a stupid mistake. He lost a finger because of it, and we could lose our lives, and the lives of everyone on this project."

Michelle jumped to her feet, pushing her light into Roselli's face, but stopped short of defending Hank. She knew Roselli was right. It *had* been a stupid mistake, and they couldn't afford stupid mistakes.

She turned her light and attention away from Roselli's icy stare.

"I'll be okay," Hank assured Roselli. "Just give me a few minutes."

"We don't have 'a few minutes,'" Roselli reminded him. "And we can't drag you along, you've already held us up too long. You'll have to go back."

Pig-nose Tony had been very quiet throughout the whole thing. He had a scholarly look on his face, as if he was about to solve world famine, or refute Einstein's Theory of Relativity. He broke his silence in a high screech of a voice. "This could be one of them invasions from another planet, or something." He looked cautiously down the duct leading to Level Two, and whispered, "Maybe there's giant ants in there and they'll eat up the whole world."

"In the first place, Tony," Riceman started, "any ant big enough to eat the world isn't going to fit in that damned duct. And as for Martians trying to take over the world, if they're dumb enough to start out in this godforsaken place, they're too dumb to worry about." Riceman was really getting the hang of it. He decided to continue. "It's very possible that the hole in the mesh was made by a group like us, coming from Level Two."

Tony pulled back as if Riceman was trying to "invade" his mind. "What about that stuff that ate Hank's finger? You ain't gonna tell me that stuff didn't come from Mars!"

Riceman had a long-standing theory that all surfers had saltwater for brains. Tony wasn't doing anything to alter that theory. Riceman looked for help, but the others were all talking to Hank.

"The government has crap you wouldn't believe," Riceman tried to explain. "Maybe it's something new they've been experimenting with on Level Two. We don't know half of what's going on in this place."

"So," Tony replied with an "if you're so smart" tone, "if some guys from Level Two were here, where'd they go?"

"In there," Roselli answered. His light was on a large hole in the mesh guarding the back of the fan. It was a clean hole, larger than the one in the duct cover, and it went right through one of the fan blades. The gel-covered edges of the mesh continued to be eaten away.

"What's behind that fan?" Riceman asked.

Brenner took a section of the plans and laid them out on the ground.

"Looks like an exhaust shaft—goes a thousand feet or so straight up to the surface," he said.

"It's a way out," Wayne commented.

"Our mission isn't to get out," Roselli reminded them. "It's to get in. And there's no way we can get all the people on all the levels out that shaft before the bomb goes off."

"But the people on Level Two might already be out," Michelle said.

"I don't think so. If anyone had touched that jelly with their clothes, they would've burned up. You saw what it did to that handkerchief. I think whoever put the hole in the duct stayed in the duct and shot some of that shit on the fan, then went back to get the others."

"But if he couldn't get out of the duct, how will the others get out?" Michelle asked. "And how are we going to get in?"

Roselli took the flamethrower from Brenner, motioned everyone back from the duct, and hit the goo with a shot of fire that turned it to ash.

"Brenner will lead the way from now on. If we find more goo at the other end, he can take care of it."

"What about Hank?" Roy asked.

"He's going back. Someone has to tell Saxon what we've found here. If it's a way out, Saxon will use it. Let's move!"

For the first time, Riceman began to understand the military, and what it was all about. It was choosing to risk your life when safety was only few feet away. He would have liked to think he would have made the same decision even if Roselli had not been there, but he wasn't sure.

Just before his turn to enter the duct, Riceman let his light fall on Hank's severed finger. Everything had been eaten except the bone. It was an oddity. The stuff could eat through metal, but not bone.

TIME	:	0224
AREA	:	CHURCH OF REDEMPTION (ROOM R11)
LEVEL	:	1
SENSORS	:	406–09

SAXON STOOD IN THE BACK OF THE TINY CHAPEL AND watched Doctor Haddon praying at the altar. Having found Haddon, Saxon needed a moment to control his seething anger after the frustrating search. The entire room was done in red velvet and gold lamé. The walls and the ceiling were mirrored, "to reflect the soul," as Haddon put it. The ornate altar was entirely gold leaf, with an occasional silver chalice. It was Doctor Haddon's New Christian Church of Everlasting Redemption. It reminded Saxon more of a whorehouse.

It was meant to replace the three Old World churches on Level Two. A few people came the first day, then the crowd grew as the joke spread, but now no one came. Doctor Haddon was left alone with his prayer.

"Jesus is love," Saxon shouted like a television evangelist.

Haddon whipped around and pointed a condemning finger at Saxon. "Sinner!" The doctor looked like something straight out of Becket, or Fun World. The heavy red velvet robe swirled about his gold suit.

"Yes, father," Saxon said as he kneeled, "I have sinned. Is it too late for me?"

The harsh lines in Haddon's face disappeared, and were replaced by those of forgiveness.

95

"It is never too late to take Jesus as your Savior, my son," Haddon assured him.

"The Devil has lead me astray. I have walked an evil path and I am tired." Saxon wondered if that was a bit too strong, but he could see by the light in Haddon's eyes he was on the right track.

"Redemption is not easy, my son," Haddon tested.

"I know, father. But it is the only way. People are going to die because of me, and I need your help to stop it. Will you and God help me?" Saxon was careful to put Haddon first, and God last. He knew that would please the doctor.

"What is it you desire, my son?"

"I need to talk with you and God."

A frown crossed Haddon's face. He stepped behind the golden altar and put his hand on the silver Bible. "God does not talk to mortal men!" he proclaimed.

"I know that, father. But I know a way to talk to God." The bait was out. Saxon waited for a tug on the line.

"What way?" Haddon asked, like the kid who wanted to see how the magician pulled the rabbit out of the hat.

"God talks to BRUCE," Saxon said.

"God talks to a computer? Do you mock Him?" Haddon was upset, but he couldn't help taking a little nibble.

"No, father. God gave man the ability to create computers so that he might talk with Him. It is written. John 3, Psalm 24." Saxon didn't know a damn thing about the Bible, but he was certain Haddon didn't either.

"That's right, my son. I know the passage well. 'AND GOD SHALL TALK TO MAN THROUGH MAN'S LABORS AND MACHINES—AND COMPUTERS.' It is written."

Saxon set the hook and started reeling.

"BRUCE is waiting for us," he said. "He has a message from God."

"God will not talk to a sinner, even through a computer. Let us cleanse your soul. Then we will go to BRUCE.

"Kneel, my son. Bend your head in prayer, and God will hear you. He will send down his swift sword of virtue to free your soul."

Saxon knelt and bent his head. From behind the altar, Haddon pulled a long silver sword with a jeweled handle, raised it over his head, and brought it down with the vengeance of God on Saxon's neck.

THE TRIP DOWN THE DUCT TO LEVEL TWO TOOK LONGER THAN anyone expected. The motionless air was quickly heated by their bodies. It grew stale and heavy, clinging to their lungs like thick syrup. The frequent sudden dips in the duct as it worked its way downward made progress hopelessly slow. Only the sporadic mutterings from Tony about monsters and the "blob" offered welcomed moments of comic relief.

As they had expected, the end of the duct was covered with the goo. They waited while Brenner purified the opening, then squeezed themselves one by one out of the duct into the welcomed light of Level Two.

Riceman was the last one to emerge from the tube, but the first to notice something was wrong . . .

TIME	:	0238
AREA	:	SECURITY COMMAND (ROOM A3)
LEVEL	:	1
SENSORS	:	613–15

SAXON SLAMMED THE DOOR, LOCKED IT, AND WALKED BRISKLY to the glass box.

"Oh, it's you," BRUCE commented. "I can tell by the way you slam the damn door!"

"Don't get smart," Saxon warned, "or I'll punch in your goddamn discpacks."

"Please, anything but that," BRUCE replied loudly.

"Get MERLYN."

"Is Doctor Haddon with you?"

"He's here, but he doesn't want to talk to you!"

"Your ten minutes were up a long time ago. Now, we'll have to start all over again. Voiceprint check, please," BRUCE demanded.

"I told you he doesn't want to talk to you. Don't make him mad. He can have you replaced with a Series 2000. You're getting too fucking old for this job anyway!" Saxon shouted.

"OK, OK. No need to get nasty," BRUCE sulked. "I'll just do the crummy fingerprint check. But I'll put on the record that it's under duress and against my better judgment."

"You better think less about your judgment and more about your fucking ass," Saxon warned as he put his hand on the glass.

"Get your pukey hand off my glass!" BRUCE yelled. "I

99

already have your greasy prints. Remember? Or are you getting so old you're losing your memory? I want Doctor Haddon, please."

Saxon unsnapped the briefcase, took out Haddon's bloody right hand, and slapped it down on the glass. Strands of sinew and drained veins extended from the jagged flesh of the stub—marking the difference between a hand severed with a surgeon's knife, and that of one torn from a struggling victim. The last few drops of blood dripped onto the glass.

"What's that on the glass?" BRUCE asked angrily.

"The last of Doctor Haddon's tears," Saxon explained.

TIME	:	0241
AREA	:	CORRIDORS ON LEVEL TWO*
LEVEL	:	2
SENSORS	:	1111–16; 1118

"WHERE IS EVERYONE?"

No one else repeated Riceman's question, but they were all thinking it. The question had come to him instantly when he saw they were alone, very. Not that he expected a welcoming committee; but Brenner had made one hell of a lot of noise with that damned flamethrower, and then the vent came loose and hit the floor like a bolt of lightning on a tin roof. The sound knocked a filling out of Riceman's tooth; and no one came to see what was in the hen house. The rooms and the corridors they passed had one thing in common: they were all empty.

Tony put it best. "Real spooky, like in that classic sci-fi movie *It Came from Outer Space*—"

"Shut up, Tony," Wayne ordered. That didn't help. If anything, it added validity to what Tony had been saying all along.

"Nothing spooky about it," Roselli said. "This is the office section; of course no one's here. It's too damn early."

That made sense. Tony managed a weak smile, but decided to save the real thing for later.

---

* SINCE ALL CONVERSATION WAS PICKED UP THROUGH THE SPECIAL TRANSMITTERS WORN BY THE MEMBERS OF THE TEAM, THERE WAS NO RECORD OF WHICH CORRIDORS THEY USED.

"Shouldn't we tell somebody we're down here?" Riceman asked.

"We go straight to the kitchen and down the dumbwaiter to Level Three," Roselli snapped. "If we see someone on the way, that's a different matter. But, we aren't down here to make friends."

That ended the discussion about looking for anyone. As for finding the kitchen, everyone visited Level Two on a daily basis; it was the only level with a cafeteria. So, unless you were important enough to have your food delivered to your room, or to the executive dining room on Level One, you had to eat down there.

Of course, the guys on Level Three didn't count. They were the fanatics of the program and worked around the clock, so their food was sent down by dumbwaiter. No one ever saw a Level Three worker. They lived and slept and ate and crapped on that level. Tony called them "real spooky."

Roselli was about ten yards in front of the group, trudging down the hall with the same walk he used to cross the desert. The others were still a little uneasy, so it was fine with them if he wanted to play scout. They had crossed several intersecting corridors and were making good time, when Roselli held up his hand in the universal "stop" position and doubled back to the group.

"I went too far," he explained. "The cafeteria's down this one." He turned the group around and headed them down another corridor.

Riceman started to argue the point, thought better of it, and followed the others, slowly. He waited until they were ahead of him, then doubled back.

He knew Roselli had not gone too far. There had to be another reason for his decision to take a different route and Riceman was determined to find it out. He almost ran the last few yards to the place where Roselli had stopped so abruptly. It took him several seconds to comprehend what he was looking at.

A man in pajamas was lying in the middle of the corridor; a gun lay by one side of his head, his brains spread out on the other.

Riceman backed up slowly. Two hands caught him by his neck and twisted him around.

"I said we're not going this way," Roselli reminded him. The big man towered over Riceman, a grim expression on his face, and a look in his eyes that Riceman would not soon forget.

In that instant, Riceman remembered how skillful Roselli had been with the knife and Hank's finger. He remembered Rita, and Saxon telling him he would be working with her killer.

"He's dead," Riceman shouted.

"No shit?"

"Shouldn't we do something?"

"Like what?"

"I don't know," Riceman confessed.

"When you do know, tell me. Until then, keep your mouth shut about this. The team's getting jumpy. Let's not do anything that'll worry them." Then, releasing Riceman, he added, "Just tell them you got lost."

Riceman followed as Roselli returned to the group. The dead man was to remain Riceman's secret, but it wouldn't help long.

The first hall the group crossed shattered the last of what peace of mind they had. A young woman was hanging starkly from the light fixture. The overturned stool at her feet told the story. Everyone had the same feeling; it was a grotesque way to die, but maybe it was better than what drove her to it. Wayne handed the bag of explosives to Tony, then took out his knife to cut her down.

"Leave her," Roselli ordered.

Wayne reluctantly sheathed the knife, but couldn't take his eyes off her. The thin electrical cord had cut halfway through her slender neck. Michelle fainted and didn't revive until they were almost to the cafeteria.

"I'm sorry," she said, making an effort to stand as Roselli put her down, "I guess I wasn't ready for that."

"I hope you never are," Roselli replied.

It was the first time Riceman had seen the least bit of compassion from Roselli. The huge man steadied Michelle till she could make it on her own. Then he left her and took his position at the front of the group. Riceman was almost glad Roselli was there. Maybe a killer was what the group needed.

As they got closer to the cafeteria, the corridor became strewn with chairs, broken lamps, and debris of all kinds. There were no more people—dead or alive.

"What movie does this remind you of?" Roy asked Tony seriously.

"*Day the Earth Stood Still*," Tony answered, as he passed another empty room.

"People disappear in that one?"

"Na, they just ran away—left homes an' buildin's an' stuff empty as hell."

"Hey, look at that!" Brenner was pointing to a makeshift barricade halfway down a side corridor. Someone had thrown chairs and desks into a pile, then tried to set it on fire. But all the furniture used on the project had to be flame retardant. When the paper burned out, so did the fire. The barricade was separated in the middle, like something just plowed clear through it.

"What do you make of it?" Brenner asked Roselli.

"Looks like people went crazy down here."

"Why?" Tony asked.

"Who knows—people panic easy—maybe some damn fool talking about monster movies," Roselli said.

No one asked Tony about the movies after that; it was hitting too close to home. They stayed a little closer together and listened a little harder. No one talked the rest of the way to the cafeteria. Every vacant room was harder to take. A hundred and forty people had just disappeared—all except two. Roselli said there would probably be somebody in the cafeteria; it was the level's designated emergency meeting area. No one believed him.

TIME : 0249
AREA : CAFETERIA/KITCHEN
LEVEL : 2
SENSORS : 2113–19; 2314–27

THE CAFETERIA WAS EMPTY, BUT THERE HAD BEEN A MEET-
ing, and not long ago. Half-empty cups of coffee and partially eaten doughnuts were scattered about a grouping of
tables.

"They left in a hurry," Brenner observed.

"Maybe they did get out," Michelle ventured.

"If they did, it wasn't through the exhaust duct," Roselli
said, feeling the warmth left in a cup of coffee. "We would
have run into them. Or at least heard them if they were
going to the duct the same time we were coming here."

"There weren't more than thirty, forty here at the most,"
Brenner added, looking at the small grouping of dirty tables in the large room. "What happened to the others?"

"That's not our concern. Let's get going," Roselli ordered.

"Where's Wayne?" Roy asked.

"He went back to cut that lady down, I seen him," Tony
said.

"Why didn't you say something?" Roselli shouted.

"He told me not to . . . he gave me the explosives."

"Do you always do what he tells you?"

"I guess so."

"Well, we can't wait."

"I'll get him," Roy volunteered.

"Stay where you are. If he's still alive, he'll follow us," Roselli said.

Riceman didn't like the way Roselli said "if" he's alive. Why wouldn't he be?

"Five minutes," Roy pleaded. "That's all he'll need."

"We have to get to Level Four," Roselli said.

"We also gotta eat, man," Tony whined. "They got twenty micros in the kitchen. Five minutes will get us cheeseburgers, man."

"I can help," Roy said.

Roselli knew Tony was right; he just hated to admit it. "OK, but five minutes is it!"

It was a bad decision as far as Riceman was concerned. Five minutes didn't seem very long now because they had plenty of time. But who knew what they would run into later. Five minutes could make the difference between bomb and no bomb. Besides, who could eat?

"I'll take a double," said Roy.

"Lots of cheese on mine," ordered Brenner.

"Hold the pickles, heavy on the ketchup." That was Roselli's order, and Riceman considered it in bad taste. He was resigned to the fact that he and Michelle were teamed up with a bunch of animals.

"I'll help," Michelle said. "I'm starving."

"By the time you get this thing organized, five minutes will be up!" Riceman heard himself saying.

"Then help," Roselli said. "You get the meat out of the freezer."

"And make Wayne a triple cheeseburger, heavy on everything," Roy added as the three of them disappeared into the kitchen.

Tony pointed to a gigantic freezer door and asked if Riceman needed help opening it.

"I can open a door," Riceman said. "I may not have all my brains in my biceps, but I am capable of doing things like picking up a telephone, opening letters, and getting into a refrigerator!"

They were all going mad, Riceman reflected, certain that he was losing control. People were dead, there was a bomb, *and* all everyone wanted was to have a goddamn cheeseburger! They were all out of their goddamn collective mind.

He slammed the refrigerator door behind him and stood looking at the long rows of hanging beef and head-high packages of unmarked meats. The buckles on his straps frosted up, and his hands began to swell. Great, Riceman thought, just what he wanted to do; fool around in some damned freezer, looking for raw hamburger meat until his fingers froze off.

His search became frantic. He couldn't leave without finding the hamburger, but he was definitely beginning to warm up; that was a sure sign of freezing to death.

He worked his way towards the back of the room, bending over the unmarked packages that lined the wall, while his hips bumped against the sides of beef. He tore the packages open and did what he could to keep the hanging beef from freezing his balls off. At the back of the room, naturally, he found several boxes plainly marked HAMBURGER PATTIES. At the same time he grabbed one of the boxes, something grabbed him.

The huge arms encircled him in a bear hug. It had a large frosted knife in one hand and arms that were cold as death. Killed by a goddamn hamburger he didn't even want. His arms were pinned to his sides. The knife pointed at his throat.

"I was going to pay for them," he explained.

There was no response; just a moan. Riceman chanced a shuffle step to the side. The knife didn't stick him. Another moan. He continued shuffling towards the door, while the monster hung on his back like some great fallen tree.

He reached the door, but he couldn't open it. He looked out the small window in the door and could see Michelle and Tony distractedly organizing buns and dressings and getting the slices of cheese laid out in a perfect row.

"Hellllp!" Riceman yelled.

They didn't hear him through the thick glass, but the thing on his back did. It moaned again and moved the knife point closer to his throat. Riceman decided it wasn't a good idea to yell. He wondered how long Michelle and

Tony would go on before they discovered something was wrong. Not that Riceman expected them to miss him, God forbid they should have the least concern about his life flashing before his eyes, but they would need the goddamn hamburger!

Michelle passed in front of the glass three times before looking up to see the frost hanging off his eyelashes. She opened the door, screamed, and the thing lunged forward, knocking Riceman, the box of hamburgers, and Michelle to the floor.

The fall broke Riceman free. He scrambled to his feet and pulled Michelle to safety.

"Shoot him!" Riceman yelled at Tony. "Shoot the sonofabitch!"

Tony didn't have a weapon, but Roy, Brenner, and Roselli rushed in with their guns drawn. The man was lying face down. He didn't move when Roy prodded him with his foot. Roselli took the knife out of the man's hand and rolled him over.

"He's dead," Roselli announced after careful examination.

"What do you mean 'dead'?" Riceman asked, taking a cautious step forward. "He just tried to stick that knife through my Adam's apple!"

"Probably just trying to get your attention," Michelle suggested.

"He sure as hell got it! What was he doing in there anyway?"

"We'll never know," Roselli stated as he got up.

Roy bent over the body. "Must've been scared real good to make him freeze himself like that. Look at his eyes . . ."

"He seen somethin' I hope I never see," Tony said.

Tony had a way of uttering one old horror movie cliché after another.

Dead bodies were becoming a common sight. This one was just pulled into the freezer, and life went on as if a dead fly had just been swept under a rug. Michelle and Tony finished the burgers—heavy on the ketchup for Roselli—and everyone gobbled them down. Everyone except

Wayne; his triple cheeseburger with everything would have gone to waste if it weren't for Riceman.

"Let's go," Roselli ordered, popping the last of the hamburger into his mouth.

"What about Wayne?" Roy asked.

"We've waited too long now. He knows the route." With that, Roselli opened the dumbwaiter door and ushered Brenner and his flamethrower in. Just before he shut the door, he gave Brenner some encouraging instructions. "There's an intercom down there. If you run into anything, let us know."

Brenner didn't get killed. Roy went next, followed by Tony. When Michelle went, Riceman realized he was alone with Roselli. He also realized that, the way things were going, he could disappear and no one would wonder why. He pulled at his earlobes and casually glanced over at Roselli.

To Riceman's horror, Roselli had pulled out his knife and was sticking it in a tabletop. Some people doodle, or bite their nails; Roselli played with his knife.

The bright lights of the kitchen danced off the chrome blade. Riceman studied the knife as it plunged again and again into the table. It wasn't an ordinary knife, like for cutting cheese or a roast. It was made for one purpose—to kill things. The blade was long: thick on top to give strength, thin on the bottom to give a razor-sharp edge. The handle was plain, carved to fit Roselli's hand, and sported what looked to Riceman to be a set of brass knuckles, through which Roselli's fingers secured their grip.

"Nice job you did on Hank," Riceman said. "Quick thinking. You're very good with a knife."

Roselli looked up from the table. "Good?" he laughed, running his finger over the blade gently so the razor edge would not cut his leathery skin.

"What's the joke?" Riceman asked, stalling till the dumbwaiter returned and he could rejoin the group.

"Nothing," Roselli explained. "Nothing funny about it. I've done a lot of things with this and I can't think of one that was 'good.'" Roselli started toward him. "Now it's your turn."

"What do you mean?" Riceman gasped as he backed away.

Roselli pointed the knife at him. "Your turn to go down."

Riceman turned to see that the dumbwaiter had arrived. He hurried in.

"Don't forget to send it back," Roselli said, cleaning his fingernails with the sharp point of the knife.

TIME	:	0316
AREA	:	SECURITY COMMAND (ROOM A3)
LEVEL	:	1
SENSORS	:	613–15

LIGHT FROM THE VIDEOSCREEN FILTERED OUT INTO THE dark room, giving a blue cast to the shadowed figure in the chair.

MERLYN was in operation, and that gave Saxon the ultimate power to decide how BRUCE's energy would be used. The videos in Security Command had already been ordered shut off, as well as those throughout the structure. BRUCE was in Saxon's hands now, and Saxon reveled in the new power.

MERLYN was the code name for the giver of secrets. One of those secrets was direct access to the "black box." Saxon could hear everything that Roselli's team said, and through computer interpretation of background noises, know everything they did.

Voice commands to BRUCE were possible, but not from Saxon. BRUCE would not recognize the metallic voiceprint, so Saxon was forced to use the keyboard console that connected the two seats in the center of the room.

As the screen flashed its messages, Saxon's hand rested on the console. Extending from the sleeve was a gray, blistered thing that only resembled a hand by the number of fingers it had. It moved more through command than through muscle and sinew. Unlike the Belium hand, it was drawn and aged, and no life flowed through it, not even artificial life. Saxon commanded, and the hand moved, or the arm moved. One of the dead fingers twitched and the screen went black.

For a long while, Saxon didn't think about the mission or the team or the project. He thought about himself. About the grand experiment. About the theory of evolution and change and life everlasting. He thought about the first girl he had ever loved and the last one he had hated. He searched his mind for other familiar memories, but they had become faded and hopelessly lost in a maze of Belium nerve fibers.

He sat alone in the darkness, waiting for that final numbing cold to fully engulf him, to send him home forever.

```
TIME     :  0319
AREA     :  UNAVAILABLE
LEVEL    :  3
SENSORS  :  1112–16; 1118
```

THE DUMBWAITER STOPPED ON LEVEL THREE WITH A JOLT. The door slid open and Riceman emerged with the grace of a camel climbing a tree.

"What's going on down there?" The voice came from a small speaker beside the dumbwaiter.

Roy pressed the button and shouted into the speaker like it was a hollow tube, "Riceman was showin' us some ballet steps!"

"Quit jacking off and send the damn thing back!" Roselli tried to sound menacing, but his voice lost something exiting from the two-inch speaker. Still, Roy didn't loose any time closing the door and sending the dumbwaiter back up.

It would take sixty seconds for it to reach Level Two, fifteen seconds for Roselli to load himself, and another sixty seconds back to Level Three. The entire process had started with Brenner fifteen minutes ago, and he was getting anxious to get on with the damned trip. Waiting for Roselli's descent seemed like an eternity.

Finally, the red light over the door turned green, Roy slid it open, and a disgruntled Roselli climbed out.

"I was beginning to think you'd gone on without me," he joked.

Riceman was about to make a wisecrack, when gunfire blurted from the small speaker.

"Wayne," Roy observed. He closed the dumbwaiter door

and pushed the return button. The red light over the door glowed intensely.

The firing stopped, and Roselli pushed the speaker button. "Wayne?"

The answer came blasting back, "Who'd you expect? Kirk Douglas? Where the hell is the dumbwaiter?"

"On its way. What's going on up there?"

No reply, just more firing. Riceman could tell by Roselli's actions that he'd rather be up there.

"Wayne?" Roselli shouted.

"Sorry, I'm too fucking busy to come to the phone, you may leave a message at the sound of—" the strained message was cut short by another round of gunfire, followed by the sound of someone getting into the dumbwaiter.

"He's on his way," Tony shouted.

"Something's on its way," Roselli exclaimed as he grabbed the flamethrower from Brenner and pointed it at the door.

The others took places in a semicircle around the dumbwaiter. Short blasts of golden flame shot from the thrower as Roselli tested it. His forehead was the only one that didn't have beads of sweat. This was what he was born for—to kill.

The last few seconds pushed the tension to the breaking point. Brenner stood by the door, his hand ready to slide it open, his feet ready to take him clear of the flamethrower if needed. Riceman didn't have a weapon, but he didn't edge away.

The red light over the dumbwaiter turned green, and Brenner jerked the door open.

Wayne fell halfway out. Every ounce of flesh was stripped from his head. The empty skull was bleached dry. The hollow eyes stared at them. There was a crackling sound and they could see the flesh being eaten away from his neck.

Michelle screamed, Riceman weakened at the knees, and both Roy and Tony froze. Roselli squeezed the trigger and a searing flame shot from the thrower. It blackened the skull, and the crackling stopped. The acrid smell of burnt flesh filled their lungs.

The green light turned red as the dumbwaiter tried to go back to Level Two. Brenner grabbed the door, pulled Wayne out, and held the door so the dumbwaiter could not go up. Roselli was already fixing an explosive charge he ripped from the bag. Not a word passed between them, but Brenner held the door until Roselli set a timer for sixty-three seconds and threw the charge into the dumbwaiter.

They ushered the group out of the room and waited by the door as they looked at their watches.

Roselli counted it, "Sixty-two—sixty—"

There was a tremendous explosion. A split second later, the dumbwaiter door blew off and smoke belched into the room.

"We gave something a hell of a ride," Brenner laughed.

"In case we didn't," Roselli said, "let's get out of here."

There were no laggards this time. The men were bigger, but Michelle was faster. She caught Riceman by the shoulder and pulled herself past him. She missed the turn and was halfway down the wrong corridor when she heard Roselli's voice booming after her.

"Hold it! You're going the wrong way!"

She didn't say anything; just reversed direction. The main group was going down another hall, but it didn't take her long to catch them. Riceman pulled over just in time to keep from being trampled as she passed. They ran across the entire length of Level Three before stopping in front of a steel door marked EXECUTIVE BATHROOM.

"It's a joke," Roselli told them, as he placed his hand on a glass device to check the prints. When he didn't hear BRUCE's obnoxious voice through the speaker, he set a charge on the door and blew it open. The blast knocked out all the lights in the area; all except the battery-powered security light that blinked a frantic red eye at them as they ran into the room. It seemed to be saying, "Uncleared people entering! Violation! Violation!" Riceman never ceased to amaze himself. After all he had been through—and everything that he would probably have to endure in the near future—he could still look at the blinking red light and wonder if he was going to be reprimanded. It only crossed his mind for an instant, but it was there.

The huge room was in total darkness, except for the times the red light lit it up like a strobe.

"Blew the lines," Roselli said.

"Where are we?" Michelle asked.

She didn't get an answer. An alarm bell went off like an aboveground fire station. Riceman was sure its function was to deafen any intruders.

Brenner quickly reclaimed his toy, went over to the bell, and silenced it with one fiery blast from his fiery dragon.

He was cradling the flamethrower in his arms when he returned to the group. "And it can cook too!" he said proudly.

Michelle had not forgotten her question. "Where are we?" she asked again.

Roselli tried to point out the highlights of the room by keeping time with the light. "There's a—laser—there's a—cyclo . . ." He gave up. "It's a lab," he said. That satisfied everyone. He moved across the room with the ease of familiarity. The rest of the group tagged after him like chicks after a mother hen.

When Riceman first saw it, it reminded him of a Fourth of July sparkler—showering sparks. It was too bright to look at straight on; it left a yellowish streak behind as it flew through the air. It struck Tony on the chest, just below the heart. His midsection blew across the room. It all seemed so unreal to Riceman in the blinking red light. Tony didn't even scream. He just sort of disappeared; knocked into the shadows by the force of the blow, tumbling after his guts like a child chasing a bag of spilled marbles.

Riceman was mesmerized by the surrealistic scene. He was still transfixed when Roselli tackled him.

"I said drop!" Roselli shouted.

"Did you see anyone?" Brenner asked from behind a steel girder.

"No," Roselli answered.

Another sparkler shot through the air, whizzed past Roselli's head, and blew a hole in the wall. With one shot, he knocked out the red light and plunged them all into total darkness.

Riceman couldn't see his hand in front of his face. He felt around, but Roselli was gone. The sparklers continued to fly, going wild. Anyone who talked ran the risk of a shot in their direction. Silence. No one even dared move. The slightest noise could be their last.

It was hard to see where everyone was, but Riceman used the light from the sparklers as best he could. Then, the worst possible thing happened: the sparklers stopped coming. Whoever it was had decided to let one of them make the first move. It was a stalemate. Roselli needed those sparklers to locate the maniac. Riceman reached in his pocket and pulled out a handful of lemon drops. He held his buckles with one hand to keep them from jingling, and threw with the other. As the candy drops landed in a far corner of the room, fireballs followed. He was down to his last lemon drop, when he heard the scream.

Another couple of minutes of silence and a single white emergency light turned on. Riceman could see Roselli walking towards him from the far side of the room.

"Crazy as hell," Roselli said.

Not ten feet away from Riceman on the floor was the revolver Tony was carrying when he got hit. It had been Wayne's; then it was Tony's; and it could have been Riceman's if he had just noticed it. He felt dumb as hell having thrown lemon drops when he could have been a real help with the gun.

"Good work," Roselli said, putting away his knife. "If you hadn't drawn his fire, I might never have found him. You got him, got him good."

"Who the hell was he?" Brenner asked.

"A lab tech," Roselli replied. "Never did like him. Squirrelly, went off the deep end."

"He got Tony," Roy said.

"Too bad," Roselli commented. "That means we're down to five. At this rate, we're going to need everyone we've got."

Numbers, Riceman thought. That's all they were to Roselli. Objects to be used up like so many bullets. Don't use too many too fast or you could run out. But maybe it took a man like him to slit another man's throat—or Rita's.

"Good work." That's what Roselli had said. And, for a while, Riceman had been proud to have helped kill a man. He wondered what he would be proud of next?

"Over here," Roselli ordered.

It was a large dome. Three feet high and nine across. There was a device on top of it, periodically shooting a beam of light through a hole that opened and closed for that purpose.

"This thing is fifty feet deep. Ends about two feet from the air duct for Level Four," Roselli explained.

Painted on the side of the dome in large red letters, was a clear warning:

EXTREME DANGER!
DO NOT REMOVE COVER!
EXTREME DANGER!

Roselli hopped up on the dome and pulled the plug on the device. Then he got down and started unsnapping things around the base.

"It says you shouldn't do that," Riceman warned.

Roselli didn't even look up; he just kept twisting and pulling and unscrewing bolts until he was sure the dome was free to move. Then he mounted an electric forklift, drove it over to the dome, and maneuvered the forks through two rings on the top of the dome.

"Oh," he said as an afterthought, "you better get behind that shield over there." He pointed and they scrambled to safety. "No telling what's in this thing." With that last warning, he began to lift the dome.

It took only a crack between the dome and the floor to change the semidark lab into the greatest light show on earth, and he had a front-row seat. It was hypnotic; sharp and vibrant light beams flew around the room like shooting rainbows.

As the dome was raised higher, Riceman stepped from behind the shield. The light grew more intense, the colors flew faster, and he was a part of it. He was life—he was God.

"Get the hell behind the shield!" Roselli shouted.

Riceman heard the warning the same time a blue beam of light passed through his left earlobe like a tenpenny nail. He made a dive for the shield as another beam took off the heel of his shoe.

As Roselli backed the dome away from the light well, golden beams shot through the air, smashing into walls and machines like artillery shells. Roselli tilted the dome in front of the forklift like a giant catcher's mitt, and waited for the fireworks to stop. When it was over, he jumped down from the forklift and peered into the hole as if nothing had happened.

The colored beams were replaced by a steady white light emitting from the hole in the floor. Riceman and the others waited for a signal from Roselli, then ventured cautiously towards him.

"What in God's name was that?" Brenner asked.

"Beats the hell out of me," Roselli answered, in a tone that showed a total lack of interest.

Riceman was holding his ear and wincing in pain when he heard Roselli's answer.

"You mean you opened this thing without knowing what was inside?" Riceman asked incredulously.

"How else was I going to find out?"

"You could have killed us!" Riceman shouted. The pain was growing—he couldn't feel anything except the throbbing.

"I took a chance," Roselli said, shrugging the whole thing off as he turned away.

The anger shot through Riceman, blinding him to Roselli's physical superiority. He jumped on the big man's back, screaming incoherently, and was quickly tossed to the floor.

"What's wrong with you?" Roselli asked, looking down at him.

"You could have killed all of us!" Riceman shouted up.

"Would you rather melt?" Roselli didn't wait for an answer. He had work to do.

Riceman suddenly realized Roselli was right: they were all dead if they didn't abort the binary bomb. Life didn't exist for any of them outside that structure. The past didn't matter, and the future didn't exist. Everything was now. No one got a free ride. And there was no sense holding back, or even being cautious; it was too late for that.

As Riceman got to his feet, he resolved not to be a bystander any longer. He was part of a dwindling team, and he would do his share.

Everyone was gathered around the hole, looking into it, but not understanding what they were seeing. Riceman found a place and gawked with the rest of them.

The well was fifty feet deep and lined with glass. At least it looked like glass, but it radiated a pure white light. Long fingers of glass jutted out towards the middle, and reminded Riceman of the Death Hoop of Knives that circus daredevils jump through; only these knives were crystal prisms and the hoop was forty-five feet deep, ending in a glass bowl. The clearance down the middle was about three feet across.

"I was here when they built it," Roselli said. "Those prisms are sharp as razors."

"Can we knock 'em off?" Roy asked.

"Try it," Roselli answered. He knew no one would believe him without seeing for themselves.

Roy grabbed a heavy pipe, stood on the edge of the hole, and slammed the pipe down like a sledgehammer. The prism didn't even move.

"Made from a new plastic," Roselli explained.

"What do they do with this thing?" Brenner asked.

"It's a laser-propulsion unit—kind of an engine."

"I thought you didn't know what it was?" Michelle said.

"I knew how it was made," he admitted. "I didn't know what was going to happen when I took the lid off." He looked around at Riceman. "Any more questions?"

"What do we do now?" Roy asked.

"I have to get down there and blow a hole in the bottom," Roselli answered.

"Can't you just drop the stuff down there?"

"No. It's a special deal," Roselli explained as he emptied the explosives sack on the floor. He picked through the mess, and then put a detonator, two units of plastic explosives, and a long tube back in the sack. Then he jumped on the forklift, dropped the dome cover, fastened a pulley to one fork, ran a thin line through it, and positioned the fork over the hole.

Riceman looked at the line running through the pulley. He didn't know anything about things like that, but it looked too weak.

"Sure that will hold you?" he asked Roselli.

"Thousand-pound test," Roselli explained.

"What if you get killed?"

"Good thinking. I better explain this whole thing to everyone." They gathered around as Roselli emptied the sack again. Pointing to the long tube, he said, "That's a special device. Designed to blast straight down, then out. It'll dig a hole big enough for you to get through. It should tear a hole in the air duct too. In case it doesn't, use those tin snips." He pointed to a pair of shears on the floor with the extra explosives. "You have to set this thing up carefully. Red end down. Has to be vertical—pack those plastic explosives around it for support. They'll help clear the area of debris. Connect the detonator wires like this—set the timer like this—push the red button and get the hell out of there. Everybody got it?" They all nodded weakly. "Good. Now, if I get killed before I can set up the charge, you won't feel so bad."

He walked around the hole and chalked a big X on the floor close to the edge. "The charge has to be set flat against the side of the chamber, fourteen inches from the bottom, in line with this spot. You can be off a little, but not much. The charge should blow a hole through the wall of the chamber into an air duct."

"And if it doesn't?" Michelle asked.

Roselli didn't answer. His silence told everyone they had one shot at it—and what would happen if it failed.

Brenner reached out across the chamber, grabbed the thin line hanging from the steel fork, ran it through a special holder, and took a position on the opposite side of the forklift. From there, and with the special holder, he could raise and lower even the largest of men.

Roselli snapped the other end of the line to his belt, tested the pulley, and gently swung out over the chamber.

His legs automatically tilted forward and he started an uncontrollable spin.

"Won't work. I have to hang straight."

Roy and Riceman pulled him back, readjusted the line just below his neck, and swung him out again. This time Roselli didn't start to spin, but still hung at a slight angle. Inspecting the line, he decided it was the best that could be done. With the bag of explosives attached to the wire above his head, he began the long descent, using his boots against the prisms to stop any sway. He didn't start to spin again until he reached the last four feet, when he ran out of prism for his feet to play against.

He checked his watch when he reached the bottom. Two minutes twelve seconds. Going down was easy; all Brenner had to do was feed out the line. The trip back up would take longer. Roselli positioned the charge, connected the detonator, set the timer for five minutes, and was on his way back up.

Brenner was better than Roselli had expected. The trip up was fast and smooth. Then, just as Roselli's head cleared the top of the chamber, the pulley jammed.

"Eighty-seven seconds," Roselli announced.

Brenner handed the wire to Roy, and climbed out on the fork, but couldn't get the pulley unjammed.

"Won't move!" he shouted.

"Then get the hell out of the way," Roselli shouted. "The blast will blow you to bits if you stay out there." Then, looking at his watch, "Twenty-three seconds."

Riceman jumped on the forklift. It was made in Japan, or Taiwan, or some damn place where they just used arrows instead of words.

"Up, up, up, up," he kept saying over and over.

He looked at Brenner, but he was too busy with the line to be of any help.

"Which arrow?" Riceman shouted.

"The one that points up!" Brenner shouted.

"Ten seconds," Roselli reminded him.

There were two arrows that pointed up. Riceman didn't know which one meant "up" and which one meant "forward." If he chose the wrong one, he would cut Roselli to pieces. BUY AMERICAN flashed across his mind as he pushed one lever.

The forks went up and so did Roselli. As soon as he could, he lifted his legs clear of the chamber and shouted, "Three seconds."

Riceman punched the other arrow, turned the wheel, and Roselli cleared the chamber just as a tremendous blast shot debris from the hole like a blunderbuss. It knocked Brenner off his feet and blew Riceman out of the seat, leaving Roselli taking a ride like a puppet on a string. Michelle leaped on the forklift, hit the brake, and stopped Roselli from getting a close look at the inside of a cyclotron.

Riceman sat on the floor listening to the crescendo of bells ringing in his head. He glanced up to see Roselli shouting something down at him.

"What?" Riceman asked, as the bells became muted horns.

"I said," Roselli shouted, "how did you know which arrow to push?"

Riceman smiled. "I took a chance."

He expected Roselli to offer a hand up, or some slight hint of appreciation. None. Well, maybe one. The hard glare that seemed to be built into his eyes disappeared for an instant, then he was gone. Riceman considered that a just reward for saving a killer's life.

He didn't get up. The bells had almost stopped, but there was a shaking inside him, a cold pulsation that kept reminding him how close he had been to . . .

He shook away the thought and concentrated on Roselli and Brenner fixing the pulley. It took a while, but they were finally satisfied they had done all they could to insure it wouldn't stick again. While they placed the fork back over the hole, Riceman noticed Michelle was sitting beside him. He didn't know how long she had been there, but her soft presence put an end to worrying about himself.

"That was quick thinking," she said, touching his shoulder.

"Another second and—"

"But it wasn't another second," she reminded him. "You saved his life."

Riceman knew she was right. He had saved Roselli's life. But that knowledge wasn't a comforting thing to think about. Rita's memory kept tugging at his mind, reminding him what Roselli was really like. Riceman wondered if it would've been better for everyone if he had let Roselli die.

He got up to watch Brenner being lowered into the chamber by Roselli.

"See how he uses his feet against the prisms?" he asked Michelle. She nodded. "That's how he keeps from spinning," he explained. Riceman knew she had seen Roselli doing the same thing and didn't have to explain it to her, but the thought of her spinning among the razor edges forced him to say something.

Brenner made it to the bottom, unsnapped the line, and sent it back up.

"Let's go!" he shouted, after examining the blast area. There was a jagged hole leading into the air-conditioning duct. The flamethrower was lowered to Brenner and he disappeared into the duct.

"Are we going to crawl around in that duct?" Riceman asked.

"Any complaints?" Roselli asked.

"No, but if you blasted through the bottom of that duct, we could drop right into Level Four and we wouldn't have to waste time looking for a vent," Riceman observed.

"There's ten feet of concrete between the duct and Level Four."

"Hey, come on!" Brenner called. He was looking up from the hole like a gopher.

Roy was next. He pulled his cowboy hat snug and swung over the chamber. He was barely into the hole, when one of his spurs struck a prism and sent him into an uncontrollable spin. The wire snagged a prism and was severed. It was not a clean fall. Roy bounced from side to side, each time leaving a part of his body lodged among the prisms. His shrieks echoed from the chamber. When what was left of him hit the bottom in a quivering mass, his agony was ended by a shot from Roselli's gun.

Brenner appeared from the duct, pushed Roy's mutilated body aside, and yelled, "All clear, let's go!"

By the time the wire was connected to another snap, and the forklift repositioned over the chamber, Michelle had recovered enough to take her place over the crimson-stained chamber.

"Use your feet on the prisms to control yourself," Riceman urged again.

For Michelle it was a journey through the macabre. The walls of the chamber were streaked with blood. Parts of Roy were wedged between the pure crystals; an overpowering wave of nausea rose up inside her. Yet, she dared not close her eyes. She had to see her feet work off the prisms; she had to stay in control. She concentrated on what she was doing, and didn't allow her eyes to stray from her feet. She didn't let herself look down; she knew what the sight of Roy's partial body would do to her. If she fainted, she knew it would be over for her too. She wondered if she would feel pain if she let her mind slip into darkness.

Her feet touched bottom and she could feel Brenner's hands pulling her down.

"Bend down, away from the prisms," she heard him say. She bent over and he unsnapped the wire. She stepped backwards and her foot landed on something soft. Her knees weakened and she fell forward.

Brenner's strong hands caught her. "Are you OK?" he asked.

She wasn't OK, and she doubted she would ever be OK again, but she heard herself answer, "Yes, I'm OK."

Maybe it was Brenner telling her everything was going to be all right, even though she knew he was lying; or maybe it was just pride and knowing she was the only woman on the expedition that made her refuse to be the only weak link in an ever-diminishing length of chain; whatever the reason, she forced herself fully conscious.

"We have to stack the deck down here," Brenner explained. "You have to get in the duct, then crawl backwards and wait for Riceman to get in front. We'll crawl forward, so Roselli can bring up the rear. Do you understand?"

She nodded her head, but she didn't really hear anything past the part about getting in the duct and backing up to make room for Riceman. She couldn't think or retain anything; it was taking all her mental power just to block out what she had seen in the chamber. She climbed into the duct, backed up, and let the darkness close in around her.

She lost track of time; it seemed like a split second until she felt Riceman's feet gently pushing at her, telling her she had to back up some more. Next she heard Brenner clamoring in, with what sounded like the flamethrower Roselli had lowered to him. She waited for movement, then followed Riceman forward. She knew Roselli was lowering himself down the death wire, but she couldn't being herself to listen. She put her hands over her ears; she didn't want to hear any more screaming—he would have to die by himself. An eternity later, she heard him crawl in behind her, and the train started.

TIME	:	0410
AREA	:	DUCTS BETWEEN LEVELS 3 AND 4
LEVEL	:	BETWEEN LEVELS 3 AND 4
SENSORS	:	1112; 1114–15; 1118

IT WASN'T RIGHT. RICEMAN KNEW THAT, BUT HE DIDN'T know what he was supposed to do to make it right. In the past few hours, he had seen three men die violent deaths. Yet it was unreal to him. He felt very little. No. Not very little. He did feel something, but it wasn't as intense as he knew it should be. No one except Michelle seemed to be overly concerned about the deaths. Brenner had shoved Roy's body aside like so much garbage.

Maybe, he thought, that's the way it has to be. They didn't have time for remorse or reflection. There was only time for one thing—the bomb. He pushed the bodies out of his mind and concentrated on the duct.

As he crawled along behind Brenner, he tested the duct's dimensions with his hand. It was a little larger than the exhaust duct, but not so large as to allow a person to rattle around. He was getting used to being in a duct; in fact, he preferred it. He felt safer. Nothing could grab him from the side, or fall on him from above. It was like returning to the womb.

Brenner kept shining his light down the duct and sliding the flamethrower in front of him. They passed several connecting ducts, some smaller and some larger than the one they were in. Brenner noted each of them, checking his map as he went.

As he passed the entrance to a larger duct, something

reached out of the dark and yanked him in. Riceman grabbed his leg, but couldn't keep him from being dragged off.

"Go, go, go!" Roselli ordered.

Riceman crawled over the flamethrower, with Michelle right on his heels. They looked back in time to see Roselli pulling the flamethrower behind as he disappeared down the large duct.

"Back up!" Riceman shouted at Michelle, and they both backed to the large duct.

"We're coming with you," Riceman announced as he started to get in the duct.

"The hell you are," Roselli snapped, as he strapped on the flamethrower. "Get to Security Control and abort ZOMBIE. You're on your own."

Brenner's flashlight was still visible far down the duct as he fought a losing battle with whatever was dragging him away. Roselli gave the thrower one test, then went after Brenner.

"We better get going," Michelle said.

"Right," Riceman said, but paused several seconds before continuing on without Roselli.

Riceman had no idea where he was. He had left the plotting of the course to Brenner. Now, there was no Brenner, there was no Roselli, and there was no map.

"Do you have a map?" Riceman asked.

"No. Brenner had the only copy."

"We could sure use it."

"What would you do with a map if you had it?" Michelle asked. "There aren't exactly any street signs around here, and you have to know where you are to use a map."

That made things worse for Riceman. For a while he just thought he didn't know how to get to Security Control, now he realized he didn't even know where he was.

"We'll just keep going until we see something," he finally said.

"Or," Michelle added, "until something sees us."

It was a sobering thought. "We'll be all right as long as we stay out of the larger ducts," Riceman said confidently.

"Tell that to Brenner," Michelle replied.

"I didn't say we wouldn't have to be careful! We'll watch out for the large ducts. But, at least that thing can't get in this one."

"What makes you so sure?"

"You ask some of the damndest questions!" Riceman shouted. "Why don't we just give up now and save it the trouble of finding us?"

It was some time before Riceman spoke to Michelle again. He could hear her crawling after him, bitching about this and that, and stopping every now and then to complain about breaking a nail, and cursing every time her knee landed on something rough.

"Give me a break!" Riceman pleaded. "It's bad enough without you bitching every five feet!"

"Well, pardon me for living. I certainly didn't want to disturb you!"

Riceman kept moving. As long as he was moving, he felt he was making progress. The air grew heavy with moisture, giving him the feeling he was crawling through ink. He lost all track of time, so he didn't know how long they had been crawling when the damp air started to turn hot. Every inch brought another degree of heat, but he knew he could not turn back.

"It's getting hot," Michelle told him.

"Is it really?" Riceman asked sarcastically, as sweat dripped off his chin.

"What are you going to do about it?" she asked.

"Sweat," Riceman answered, continuing down the duct.

Thirty feet ahead, the duct turned sharply. Riceman moved along slowly, not sure what to expect. The air was getting hotter and, as he got closer to the bend, he could smell burnt flesh. He edged up to the bend and stopped. He didn't want to know what was around it, but he couldn't go back. Michelle started bitching about the smell, not realizing what it was, and Riceman decided that with her on his ass, he didn't have that much to lose.

He inched around the bend, holding his flashlight way out front and ready to jerk his arm back at the slightest provocation. When his arm didn't get grabbed, he stretched his neck out and peered around the corner.

Another two feet and the duct emptied into a much larger one. He couldn't see the bottom of the new duct, but he judged that a person could stand up in it. He pushed himself back around the bend and rested.

"What's wrong?" Michelle asked.

"Nothing," he assured her.

"What did you see?"

"A large duct. This one ends and starts up on the other side."

"So?" Michelle asked, with a tone that told him she really meant, "What are you waiting for?"

"Sooooo, I don't want to stick my head in it and have something grab me," Riceman explained.

"Is something there?" she asked.

"How should I know?" Riceman answered curtly.

"You didn't look?" Michelle asked, amazed.

"I didn't look!" he snapped.

"Do you want me to look?"

"No, I don't want you to look! Besides, how could you? I'm in front. You're just trying to make me feel guilty."

"No, I'm not. But I'm hot! I've got to get out of here," she said.

"OK, OK! I'll look!" Riceman exclaimed. It's marvelous, he thought, how woman inspires man.

He edged around the corner again, creeped up to the big duct, and looked in. He shined his light down one way and then down the other. Nothing. Then, he pointed the light straight down to see how to get out.

Lying on the bottom of the duct was the charred body of what used to be a man. The flesh was still smoldering. Riceman felt sick, but he couldn't turn away from the sight.

"What do you see?" Michelle asked.

"Nothing," Riceman lied.

The trick was to get out of the duct without falling on the body. He let himself go headfirst till his hands touched the bottom of the large duct, then he tumbled to one side. From what he could see as he stood beside the body, there had been a long fight. The walls of the duct were still hot from what Riceman assumed was the flamethrower. By the size of the body, he guessed it was Brenner.

"Can I get out now?" Michelle called.

"Yeah, come on."

Riceman put his flashlight in the small duct opposite the one that Michelle was in. That gave enough reflected light so he could help her out, but not enough to reveal Brenner's body. With a renewed burst of energy, he plucked her from the duct.

"Thank God, I'll be able to stand up," she said.

"No, you won't," Riceman said, carrying her to the small duct. "In you go."

"No, I don't!"

"Yes, you do!"

Riceman could tell that protecting her from Brenner was going to be a hell of a job.

"Get in there!"

"The hell I will!" Michelle shouted, holding her hands against the sides of the duct.

"You have to!" he explained.

"I don't have to do a damn thing!"

A sound like a great wounded animal echoed down the duct. Riceman dropped Michelle and grabbed his flashlight. Michelle saw Brenner, and looked up in time to see Riceman's light flash across something enormous barreling down the duct towards them. She leaped into the small duct. The thing was too far away for Riceman to see clearly, but he wasn't going to wait for a closer look. He jumped in after Michelle. Something tugged at his heel, but he managed to pull free. As he crawled away, he could hear something trying to get in after him.

Terror stricken, they crawled frantically through the steel maze of ducting until exhaustion overcame fear and they collapsed against the walls of the duct.

"What was it?" Michelle gasped.

"Shh," Riceman cautioned. He listened for some time before he felt safe. "Whatever it was, it's not following. I don't think it could get in the duct."

"Maybe we just lost it," Michelle ventured.

The thought of being lost in a maze with something that wanted to kill them was too much to bear.

"It's fast. If it could have gotten in this duct, it would have caught me. It's too big," Riceman said.

Michelle quickly agreed. The thought reassured them.

"If it couldn't get to us, why did you keep pushing me to go farther—I'm almost dead," she asked between heavy breaths.

"Me?" Riceman exclaimed. "I wanted to stop a long time ago but I didn't want to lose you—I was just following."

If they hadn't been so tired, or so scared, they might have laughed. As it was, the most they could do was smile weakly. Even that was lost in the darkness.

"Your face is dirty!" Riceman exclaimed.

"I wonder why?" Michelle snapped.

"I mean I can see your face—there's light coming from some—there!" Riceman pointed to a small vent in back of her. "It's a vent—we can get out."

"Not unless we go on a crash diet."

"Give me the bag of explosives. I'll blast us out of here."

"What bag?"

"You don't have the bag?"

"Should I?"

"Roselli dropped it when he got the flamethrower. You must've backed right over it."

"I didn't see it," Michelle explained.

"You didn't see it, or you didn't look for it!"

"Take your choice!" Michelle shouted.

"That's just great. Now what do we do?"

"Don't ask me; you're leading!" she said, tears running down her face.

Riceman didn't know what to say, so he didn't say anything. Tears were unfair; they always won. He patted her knee with a kind of "good ol' Shep" pat that didn't seem to console her.

He looked at the vent and kicked out in a rage. He rammed his foot into it four times before it fell to the floor like a hundred cymbals.

The once weak light that filtered through the mesh

cover now shined brightly through the open vent, and gave them hope. Not hope of escape through the vent, but the hope a small light brings to a dark room. Riceman could see the radiant smile that was always a part of Michelle, and he felt renewed.

He took her hand in his as they sat silently enjoying the light, and she stopped crying. He felt better than he had ever felt in his life, and he wouldn't have traded that moment for all the security in the world. He slid one leg out the vent as he moved towards Michelle. It wasn't the right time, and it sure as hell wasn't the right place; but he took her in his arms and kissed her anyway.

Pain shot through his leg as something pulled it farther out the vent. He could feel the joints start to pull apart and the tendons stretch. He was going to lose his leg, he knew it. An agonizing scream came from him, and his leg was released. He was in too much pain to move by himself, so Michelle helped pull his leg back into the vent. When they were safely away from the vent, she turned her flashlight on.

"Is it bad?" she asked, looking at the torn pant leg.

"Na," Riceman said sarcastically, clenching his teeth. "It only tore my leg half off—I'll be all right in a minute." He rubbed the leg and flexed his toes. Everything worked.

"Anything broken?"

"I don't think so, but I think there's a big gash just above my ankle," he said.

"Let me see. It's probably not as bad—oooooeee! That looks bad," she exclaimed.

"Gee, thanks," Riceman said as he forced himself to look at the wound. "Why isn't it bleeding?"

"I don't know. Sometimes deep wounds don't bleed—until later," she said confidently.

"Oh, that makes me feel a lot better."

"How's the rest of your leg feel?"

"How do you think it feels? It was damn near torn off and you expect . . ." Riceman stopped. His leg didn't feel that bad. It was a little sore, but other than that, everything was pretty good, considering.

"What's wrong?"

"Nothing," he answered. "I think I can crawl along OK. We better start looking for a larger vent."

"Sure?"

"Yeah."

As they crawled, Riceman thought. There wasn't much else to do. The flashlight had been turned off to conserve batteries, and that left them in a whole lot of dark. It was like a bad dream, or that mile-long tunnel in Zion Park he went through as a kid. Everything would be dark as hell, then there'd be a speck of light that would grow and grow until it was bigger than a house and he could see out of a window cut right in the side of the mountain. But this time the window never got bigger than a small vent and he never got to see out of anything. Once in a while, whenever they passed a vent, he could see Michelle's shapely derriere; but it didn't happen very often, so mostly he just thought.

And he thought mostly about the wound and the lack of bleeding. He would have been happier if the damn thing at least had the decency to gush a few times. A tourniquet would have been nice. It wasn't that it didn't bleed at all, there was enough to soak his pant leg; but it stopped so quick. He wondered if that was a sign of blood poisoning. His head butted Michelle in the rear and knocked her flat.

"Sorry," he said to the dark in front of him.

"Not your fault, I was driving without taillights."

They laughed, but it was a tense laugh. Michelle shined the flashlight in front of her and Riceman could see why she had stopped. The duct they were in ran straight ahead, but it slanted down at a steep angle. Off to their left, another duct ran level, but was smaller.

"I think we should stick with the main duct. At least we won't get stuck," Riceman said.

Michelle agreed and they proceeded slowly. They both knew that, because of the extreme angle of the duct, there would be no backing up; if it ran into a dead end, they would be just as dead. Before, they had been able to see light from the next vent, but not this time. The duct slanted into complete darkness, requiring Michelle to turn the flashlight on more often. They passed many smaller connecting ducts, each equally as dark and foreboding. Their duct grew smaller—too small to crawl in—and they were forced to pull themselves along with their elbows. The air was thick with moisture, and they had to fight for each breath. Sweat began running off their foreheads, and soon their bodies were wringing wet.

"I want out of here!" Michelle screamed. She pounded on the sides of the duct, and refused to go any farther.

Riceman was shocked. He had never seen her fall apart like this. She was always the super cool one with the right answers. He couldn't go back. He couldn't go forward. And he wondered how persuasive he could be talking to her rear.

"What's happening up there?" he asked calmly.

"Nothing!" she snapped.

"Are you stuck?"

"No!"

"Are you—resting?"

"No!"

"Are you—"

"Noooooooo!"

He wasn't sure what he had been going to ask her, but he was glad the answer was no. He knew the next step would be crucial. He let her calm down. When she stopped beating on the duct, he decided to try again.

"Logically speaking—"

"Screw logic!" she yelled.

So much for that, he thought. Maybe the direct approach would be best.

"What's wrong?" he asked.

"We're twelve hundred feet underground; being chased by something that wants to kill us; stuck in a goddamn air duct; sweating to death; running out of air; and about to be blown up by a fucking bomb; and you want to know what's wrong?"

There was a long period of silence, followed by a long period of hysterical laughter, followed by a long period of hysterical crying. Riceman liked the silence best.

"You'll have to excuse me," Michelle said. "It's just before my period and I'm a little on edge." Back to the laughter, then silence.

"Can you reach my pants pocket?" she asked.

He didn't know what she had in mind, but it was bound to beat the last few minutes.

"Sure," he answered.

"Would you reach in and get my compact."

My God, Riceman thought, she's gone off the deep end. Knowing he couldn't get out until she moved, he thought courtesy the best policy. It was a struggle getting into her pocket; she filled her jump suit pretty good. Once he got his hand in, it was stuck.

"Are you getting fresh?" she asked.

"No, ma'am."

"Too bad," she said with a sigh.

When he finally got the compact out, he handed it to her and she flipped it open. It had a small light that shined on her face.

"Holy Jesus!" she exclaimed.

"What's wrong?"

"My damn makeup is melting off!"

"Is that all?" Riceman said. Instantly he knew he had made a big mistake.

"Is that all?" she shouted. "Do you know how long it takes to get it on right? Just guess?"

Riceman sensed it was one of those trick questions, the kind where no answer is the best answer. He decided to wait her out. In her mood, it didn't take long.

"The damned stuff is eighteen dollars an ounce and guaranteed not to run. I'm going to write those bastards a letter!"

Riceman clutched at the opportunity.

"I'll bet there's a typewriter on Level Four. Let's find it," he offered.

"Right," Michelle answered. Snap went the compact as she started moving forward. One more bend and the duct emptied into a spacious metal tank the size of a small room.

Riceman held Michelle's feet until she touched bottom, then she helped him in. There were several ducts leading out. The floor was a heavy mesh that covered what Riceman felt must be some kind of dehumidifier. A constant whirring and churning under their feet didn't add to their feeling of safety.

"I didn't see this on any slide," he said. "Did you?"

"No."

There was a lot about the conference he didn't remember, and he had hoped this was one of them. He didn't like things that just popped up without warning.

"Why didn't Saxon tell us about this part of the system?" Riceman asked.

"He probably didn't expect us to end up here—we did get lost," Michelle reminded him.

Riceman was busy inspecting the floor with his flashlight. It was round, cut in half, and each half was connected to the wall of the tank by two pins. He wasn't very good at visual perception, but it looked to him like the mesh floor was designed to pivot on the pins—he thought of a trap door. It wasn't one of his more comforting thoughts. Cautiously, he scientifically tested the floor by stomping around.

"What are you doing?" Michelle asked, resting on the floor.

"My foot went to sleep," he explained. It was a lie, but that was better than getting Michelle excited. The floor passed the stomp test and Riceman was beginning to feel reassured. Then he heard it.

At first he couldn't place the sound, but it wasn't long before it was clear. A definite roaring of water, and it was coming from one of the ducts. Riceman looked at Michelle; she was getting a little edgy.

"I need a bath," she said, "but not that damn bad. Let's get the hell out of here!"

"Pick one," Riceman said.

"That one!" she answered, pointing to a large duct about twelve feet up.

They started climbing, using the lower ducts as steps. As the sound of the water got closer, they climbed faster, but the ducts were slippery and progress slow. Just like a woman, Riceman thought, always picking the box on the highest shelf. A sudden torrent of water shot across the tank, struck Michelle on the back, and knocked her down on Riceman.

When they hit the floor, the water was two feet deep and rising fast. Four more torrents of water shot from ducts, and they were instantly neck deep in water and swimming for their lives. They weren't the only things swimming. Huge, red-eyed rats, flushed from the ducts, were clawing for a foothold on Michelle's back. She fought at them through the garbage, but there were too many.

"Get them off!" she screamed frantically at Riceman.

He was having a hell of a time keeping his head above water. The flashlight was the floating kind, like a life preserver, but not a good one. He could hear Michelle screaming, but there wasn't much he could do about it. Kicking to the side of the tank, he managed to get into a large duct. Half in and half out, he pointed the flashlight at Michelle. Three large rats clung to her hair. She had given up trying to shake them off, and was swimming towards Riceman. The grinding sound beneath the water grew louder. A wave of panic flooded Riceman as he realized what the tank was.

"Come on!" he shouted. "Hurry!"

It was a stupid thing to say, and he knew it. She didn't need someone to get her to "hurry." She wasn't taking a leisurely bath, for God's sake.

Just as he grabbed her hand, the floor opened and everything was sucked into a giant disposal. Amid the sounds of grinding, Riceman watched in horror as Michelle's hand began to slip from his. The rats scurried over her head, up her arm, across their hands, and raced up his arm and passed his ear on their way to safety.

As suddenly as it began, it ended. The water drained from the tank, the floor closed, and Riceman lowered Michelle. They sat very quietly for a long time before Riceman spoke.

"Build a better mouse trap and . . ."

Michelle was climbing up after him with a strange look in her eyes. He decided not to wait for her. He had a head start down the duct, but she was a faster crawler and overtook him easily.

The chase had taken them farther than either had thought possible. Exhausted, Michelle rested her head on his thigh, and they lay that way for several minutes. Riceman finally reached down, stroked her hair, and tried to explain why he couldn't help her in the water.

"I can't swim," he confessed.

"I know. I've seen your personnel file."

"I'm sorry."

"You saved me and three rats. What more could a drowning man do?"

He felt good about that. In fact, he felt damn good. Better than he should feel for a half-drowned man with a bad leg. He was doing great. He didn't even feel tired. Probably the adrenaline.

Riceman shined his light down the duct. It divided. It would be much easier, Riceman thought, if the damn duct didn't keep dividing. He was getting tired of making decisions that turned out to be wrong. One duct sloped upwards at a slight angle, the other ran level. That old song about the high road and low road ran through his mind, and he wondered which one got to Scotland first. He flashed the light back and forth between them, as if it would make the decision for him.

"Which way?" he asked Michelle.

"What are the choices?" she asked, without looking.

"One is level, the other slants up."

"If I'm going to die, let me do it on the level."

"But, if we go up," he said, "we might get out of the duct quicker."

"Then we'll go up," she sighed.

"Good choice."

It made him feel better just knowing she made the choice. She could never say "I told you so." He didn't dwell on the fact that it was a life-and-death decision; *everything* was a life-and-death decision.

"Ready?" he asked.

"What if the water comes and flushes us out of here and

grinds us up in that big hamburger machine?" she asked solemnly.

"Then you get a full refund."

"Seriously."

He could tell she really didn't want to be ground up. He wondered if that wouldn't be better than what was waiting for them. At least it would be over.

"Seriously. The water didn't come out of the air-conditioning duct."

"How do you know?" she pressed.

"It couldn't have. Air ducts are vented into rooms, if water is forced through an air duct, the rooms tend to flood, bad for the carpets. Therefore, the water did not come from an air duct. We are safe, because we are in an air duct. End of report. Let's go."

There were times his logic and high I.Q. came in handy. The smug look on his face was lost in the dark. He wished she would learn to be more trusting. Sometimes a person of lesser intellect had to depend on a person of higher intellect.

"How do you know we're in an air duct?" Michelle asked.

The silence was deafening. After due consideration of all facts, he answered. "I just know."

With that fine bit of logic under his belt, Riceman started up the duct. He could hear Michelle following. He could also hear a thumping.

"Listen," he said as he stopped.

It was definitely coming from the duct they were in. He turned on the light, but the batteries were too weak to see very far. The noise was getting louder. It was something rolling down toward them, and whatever it was, it wasn't round. It was having a hard time thumping down the steep angle of the duct.

"What could it be?" Michelle asked.

"Maybe a square rat," Riceman replied.

Whatever was coming down the duct, it was picking up speed and taking bigger bounces.

"Let's get out of here!" Michelle yelled as she scrambled for the side duct. Riceman was right behind her, but he could tell he wasn't going to make it. He flashed his light up the duct as something raced towards him. Black and red, the size of a cantalope, spinning and bouncing too fast to see what it was. Michelle had entered the other duct, but Riceman was right in the thing's path. He lay flat, but it still hit his head with a mighty thump. Its speed gone, it rolled across his back and came to rest between his feet. Riceman kicked and pushed, and shined the light on it.

The duct began to spin. He felt faint and the nausea grew in his mind. The scream stuck in his throat as he looked down at Corporal Jackson's bloody head.

Riceman didn't remember getting in the duct behind Michelle and yelling for her to go. He didn't remember anything until they found the large vent. Michelle asked several times what he had seen, but he didn't answer. She was as excited as a child at Christmas over finding a vent large enough to get through, but he just lay there in the light of the vent, and tried to forget the hollow eyes and broken jaw of the man he once called friend.

```
TIME     :  0444
AREA     :  UNAVAILABLE
LEVEL    :  4
SENSORS  :  1114–15
```

A BURNING HATRED WAS GROWING WITHIN RICEMAN FOR the thing he once feared, and he wasn't going to run anymore. When he finally shoved the mesh covering off the vent, it was with a new determination. He was going to stop the bomb, but there was something new: an unsettling realization that he would kill without hesitation or remorse.

He didn't think about right or wrong, just or unjust; he was simply going to kill it. He didn't think about how he was going to do it, or even if he could. He had had enough!

Almost before the vent cover hit the floor, Riceman was out of the duct and helping Michelle down.

"We're making too much noise," she warned.

"Don't worry about it."

There was something about his eyes that kept her from questioning the logic of his statement: they were fixed and hard. He had changed, and the change sent a chill through her.

The vent had let them out in some kind of a lab: chemicals and test tubes and yards of glass tubing connecting beakers filled with unknown bubbling substances. The sterile white room with its gleaming modular tables and chrome chairs was right out of the pages of *Vogue* with a leggy beauty selling pantyhose taking the spotlight while a white-frocked chemist discovered the secret to eternal life in the background. Only this chemist wasn't as neat as

Madison Avenue would have liked. Manuals were strewn about the crisp-cornered tables like the bargain table at a secondhand bookshop. Papers overflowed plastic waste-baskets, and dirty beakers were scattered about like so many empty bottles of booze.

"Impressive as hell," Riceman said sarcastically.

There was no caution left in him. He wanted it over. He stepped into the corridor without checking it first, and made no effort to conceal his presence. He rattled about the empty halls looking for Security Control and burst into deserted rooms. When that didn't get results, he stood in the middle of the corridor and shouted out to see if anyone would answer; no one did. In frustration, he kicked in another door and bolted through it. It was another lab. Michelle found a small knife on one of the tables and threw it to Riceman.

"Do it now!" she ordered.

"What?"

"Kill me now!"

When Riceman seemed puzzled, she took his hand and pulled the knife up to her throat.

"Do it. I can't take any more," she confessed.

Riceman pulled the knife away and threw it down. "Are you crazy?"

"No crazier than you!" she shouted.

"What are you talking about?"

"The way you're acting," she explained. "You want to get yourself killed. Well, I don't want to be down here alone!" Her voice shook with fear. The color had left her face. Her hands trembled, and she quickly clasped them together.

"I'm going to kill it!" Riceman said.

"How? You don't even know what it is, or what will kill it. Or do you think all you have to do is walk up to it and say 'I am mad as hell Mister Thing, so roll over and die.' We all laughed at Tony, but I'm not laughing now! Those goddamn cylinders opened and something got out. It blew up everything on the surface and, for all we know, has killed everyone on Levels Two and Three, and I haven't seen anyone down here either. It has killed everyone in its path. Hundreds of people! And you think you're the one that's going to kill it. And what makes you think it's an 'it' and not a 'them'? There were two cylinders; that means at least two. We aren't stronger than it, and I don't know if we're smarter; but there's sure as hell no reason for acting dumber! You don't see it screaming down the hall telling us where it is! Don't just stand there! Say something!" she screamed.

"As I see things," Riceman said, "we aren't that bad off." It wasn't supposed to be funny, but a little laughter made her feel better. She couldn't hold back the tears any longer. Her body shook as she fell into his arms. Suddenly she pulled back from him, looked into his eyes, and Riceman jumped. Her beautiful eyes had run all down her face and she looked like she had two big black eyes and . . .

"I must look a mess," she said, searching for her compact.

"No you—don't—honest." The word *honest* stuck in his throat, prompting Michelle to search faster.

While she was busy, Riceman was busy searched the room for weapons. He found a baseball bat and seven razors. Not much of an arsenal, but he added it to the pocketknife Michelle found, and spread the weapons out on a table.

"Take your choice," he announced.

Michelle walked to the table, and Riceman was glad to see that her eyes were back on.

"Is that it?"

"Well," Riceman quipped, "if the knife and bat don't get it, we can shave it to death."

"Maybe we're worried about nothing," she suggested.

"I don't get you."

"Maybe it's just as afraid of us as we are of it."

"It's doing a hell of a job of covering that up."

"I'm serious," Michelle insisted.

"What about Brenner and Roselli? It wasn't afraid of them."

"Even a mouse will fight if it's cornered," Michelle explained. "Brenner practically ran into it. It was frightened, so it struck out and killed him."

"It didn't strike out, it dragged him off kicking and screaming," Riceman reminded her.

"You know what I mean."

"What about Roselli?" he asked.

"We don't know about Roselli. He could still be alive."

"Now you're going to tell me Jackson tore his own head off!"

"Corporal Jackson?" she asked.

"Yeah, it used his head as a bowling ball in the duct. Tell me about its sense of humor!"

Michelle's face paled. Riceman was sorry he told her about Jackson, but she was getting carried away. She sat down, regained her composure, and continued.

"All right, it killed Jackson, but we don't know why."

"It tore his head off!" Riceman shouted.

"So it doesn't play nice. Dead is dead! I know you're supposed to shoot everyone in the heart with sterile bullets, but maybe it doesn't kill by our rules."

"What about my leg?" Riceman asked. "Are you going to tell me it didn't really try to tear it off, it was just frightened by it?"

"As soon as you yelled, it turned you loose," she reminded him.

"Oh, good. I'll try to remember to yell when it tears my head off."

"Stop being so sarcastic and listen. If it hadn't rolled Jackson's head down that duct, you would have gone the wrong way and we would still be lost in there."

"Now I see. It used Jackson's head as kind of a road sign to steer us in the right direction. Wasn't that clever?"

"Explain this," Michelle challenged. "You've made enough noise in the last ten minutes to give it a headache, and it hasn't attacked us."

"How could we ask for a better friend?"

"OK, OK. I'm not suggesting you take it home to mother. All I'm saying is if we don't surprise it, it might leave us alone. You might have had the right idea before. Let's make a lot of noise so it will know right where we are. That way we won't frighten it."

"I have a better plan. Let's kill it, then it won't get

frightened," Riceman said. "And what about all the people it killed on the surface, and all those you were just telling me about on the second and third levels, not to mention this level?"

"The people on the surface were killed by the Belium explosion, and we only saw one body on Level Two, and that was a suicide. I just want you to keep an open mind."

"Fine," Riceman agreed, "I'll keep an open mind, and the knife. You keep the bat; you may need to hit me over the head if I get too violent with our friend. I hope . . ." Riceman stopped, raced across the room to a fire extinguisher hanging on the wall. He picked it up and carried it back with the pride of a new father.

"You can't kill it with that," Michelle commented.

"You know that, and I know that, but it doesn't know that. Look at this thing." It was a typical *cold-foam* extinguisher with a long conical tube. "It looks just like a flamethrower."

"Not to me."

"Our friend won't know any different."

"He will as soon as you pull that trigger," Michelle pointed out.

"If I have to, I will. That'll be even better. That white shit will scare the hell out of him."

"You're underestimating its intelligence," she warned.

"No," Riceman explained, "I'm hoping it will overestimate mine. I want it to think that I think this thing will kill it. A couple of squirts of foam, and it'll run like hell. Let's go find Security Control and abort ZOMBIE. I'm ready for anything."

Riceman closed the pocketknife and put it in his pocket. He grabbed the extinguisher, Michelle picked up the bat, and they both decided to leave the razor blades.

"How do we find Security Control?" she asked.

"I used to work down here on ET—on the old computer. The room is right next to Security Control, but I'm turned around. All the corridors look the same unless you know where you are," Riceman explained.

"What aisle was it on?"

"I never looked. I just got off the elevator, checked through Security, and went right in the room. If we can find the elevators, Security is right there. Come on."

THE SIGN ON THE DOOR READ:

SECURITY CONTROL
AUTHORIZED PERSONNEL ONLY

It was a big sign, almost the size of the door, and gave the impression of being the entrance to a massive security facility run by hundreds of men, instead of the two-man room Riceman knew it to be.

Jackson's headless body greeted him as he entered the small room. "Wait a minute," he said to Michelle. He pulled the body from the chair and stuffed it in a storage cabinet. The floor was hopeless. There was no way of getting all the blood off it. He stepped into the hall.

"Don't look down, and don't slip," he warned Michelle.

They entered the room and closed the door. She tried to not look down, but kept slipping in the partially dried blood. Half a comic book lay beside the desk nearest the door.

"Let's get it over with," she whispered. Whispering seemed the right thing to do in a room that still had the smell of death.

Riceman sat at the computer keyboard cracking his knuckles.

"Do you have to do that?" she asked.

148

He stopped cracking, took the instructions Saxon had given him out of the inside pocket of his jump suit, set them carefully up between the keyboard and the terminal's screen, and pulled a chair over to the desk, making sure it wasn't the one Jackson had been sitting in. He reached for the "brightness" control on the terminal unit and dimmed the screen a bit.

"For God's sake do it!" Michelle yelled.

Riceman gave her a temperamental artist's glance, sat down, and started punching the keys with the index finger of his left hand. S—I—G—N—O— He couldn't find the *N* again. "I know it's here, I just used it," he said as he searched the keyboard.

"I can't stand it! Let me do it, or we'll be here all night!" She tugged at the chair. Riceman got up slowly, but didn't stop looking for that damn *N*. Michelle punched the *N* and then the "return" key. She sat down and waited for BRUCE to reply.

Instead of asking for her name, BRUCE's reply was one word on the screen:

MERLYN

"Who's MERLYN?" she asked.

Riceman leaned forward. "MERLYN! Damn. Punch the question mark and return."

Michelle followed his orders, and the reply flashed across the screen:

ALL TERMINALS SHUT DOWN AS REQUESTED BY COLONEL C. P. SAXON.
SHUT DOWN TIME : 0402 HOURS

There was a click, and the unit turned off.

"What's MERLYN?" Michelle asked.

"It gives complete control over BRUCE to either Saxon or Haddon, but it takes both of them to activate MERLYN. I don't know why Saxon would shut us out, when he knows we need to use the terminal to abort ZOMBIE. And why would Haddon go along with him?"

"What makes you think Haddon knows what's going on?"

"I told you, it takes both of them to access MERLYN."

"Once activated, do they both have to be around, or can one of them run MERLYN?"

"It only takes one of them."

"There's your answer," Michelle said. "Saxon tricked Haddon into activating MERLYN, then took over."

"Saxon wouldn't do that."

"I realize he's the personification of virtue, but the possibility does exist."

Riceman couldn't accept that. If Saxon didn't want ZOMBIE deactivated, why did he send them down to Level Four. If the bomb went off, Saxon would be killed too! There was no logic to any of it. Riceman didn't like things that were illogical, that didn't make sense. That's why Michelle always thought of the best questions, and the best answers; she wasn't bothered by their being illogical. Could be, Riceman thought, that illogical questions need illogical answers. Michelle could be right, again.

"Well?" she asked.

"Well?" he asked cautiously.

"What now?" she asked impatiently.

"I don't know," Riceman confessed.

"That's not good enough, damnit! Do something!" Michelle shouted. The lights went off. "That's not funny!"

Riceman looked into the hall and flashed his light around. "Everything's off," he commented. His light fell on the door across the hall—A4117. "Come on," he called.

"Where to?" Michelle asked.

"ETHEL!"

```
TIME     :  0505
AREA     :  ROOM A4117
LEVEL    :  4
SENSORS  :  1114–15
```

RICEMAN STEPPED QUICKLY INTO THE DARK ROOM, PULLING Michelle in after him and slamming the door.

"Geeezus," he said, the thick, musty air choking him. "The bastards shut off the goddamn air conditioning!" His flashlight beamed around the wall vents like a dancing ball. "They shut the vents? Goddamn! They shut the vents!"

"They shut the vents," Michelle repeated with a manner that told Riceman she didn't understand anything.

For a brief moment his world was centered by the closed vents. Nothing else mattered. All that he had gone through, all the problems, all the terrifying hours leading to this moment faded into a weak shadow. His arms waved through the black air and the great ball of light jerked from its perch on the vent and raced about the room on its own, dancing around the ceiling, the floor, and the walls as he shouted.

"They control the humidity. You could swim in this goddamn air." Then, as the dancing ball flashed across her face on its way to a distant corner, he reemphasized his point. "I told 'em to leave the vents open, the humidity is too damn high!"

The volume of his exclamations drove Michelle back against the door. She spoke in a slow and deliberate manner. "It'll be all right."

Riceman sat down cross-legged on the cement floor. The fight had been drained from him in one huff of damp air. "You don't understand," he said quietly.

"No, I don't," Michelle confessed.

Riceman stopped the dancing ball from its wanderings and guided it to the many chest-high gray cabinets in the room. "This is ETHEL," he explained. "She's a computer, but she can't run in this humidity."

Michelle took the flashlight and shined it over the operator console. "A 4451," she remarked.

"ETHEL," Riceman corrected.

"I thought BRUCE was the—"

"BRUCE?" Riceman seemed to come alive with anger at the name. "He's less than five years old. When I first came here, ETHEL was all there was. She ran the whole project. Do you realize what a feat that was for a 4451— ETHEL?"

"Impossible."

"Damn close to impossible," Riceman said, getting up and crossing to the console. "But we did it. We could still do it. But when BRUCE was brought in, Haddon shut ETHEL down. He wanted to get rid of her entirely, but there's no market for a 4451. So they just turned her off and closed the damned vents."

"Doesn't really matter, does it?"

"What?"

"The vents," Michelle answered, her voice coming from the faint gray shadows behind the flashlight. "Even if the vents were open, there's no electricity. And even if her discpacks were still operational, the information on them would be out of date."

Riceman didn't like talking to a flashlight. It somehow reminded him of talking to BRUCE. He stepped to one side, out of the light beam, and stepped forward until Michelle's outline could be seen.

"ETHEL has her own backup generator. Over there." He took Michelle's hand in his and directed the flashlight to an orange button next to the door. "Hold it there," he instructed, crossing to the button. "The batteries that started the generator are kept charged by the main system." He pushed the button—chug—chug—bang—whirrrrrrr.

"Now what?"

Riceman felt the black wall for a familiar switch and snapped it. Lights.

Michelle let the flashlight fall to her side as if it weighed a hundred pounds.

"That's better," Riceman commented, squinting his eyes until they adjusted to the harsh light. He suddenly felt much better about the whole catastrophe. Light had that effect on him. "As for the information being out of . . ." He stepped behind a tall cabinet and waited for Michelle to follow. When he was sure she could see, he pointed to a black cable. "This is a direct link to BRUCE. We used it to transfer information from ETHEL's packs to BRUCE's. All I have to do is plug it in and we can access everything BRUCE knows—if the humidity was right."

"It's as right as it'll ever be," Michelle pointed out. "ETHEL might not work 100 percent, but that's better than nothing."

Riceman made his way around the room throwing switches, waiting for that slight variation in noise that would signal the end to ETHEL. When he finally reached the operator's console, everything was still humming fine. He gently pressed the red button and waited for the screen to light up.

"It isn't going to work."

"Give it a chance," Michelle said at his side.

The blank screen lit. Riceman pushed a series of instructions on the keyboard—and—

READY

The message on the screen was simple, yet direct. ETHEL was coming out of retirement.

"Can she talk?" Michelle asked, wondering if they would have to key in all the instructions.

"No. But she understands English instructions. There's no coding. Just a few passwords."

"That's it?"

"That's it. We didn't use a lot of security levels until BRUCE came on line. And the ones we did use, I programmed."

"MERLYN?"

"An old version. But I'm not interested in what was, I want to know what MERLYN knows now."

"You mean by linking up to BRUCE. Can we get past his security monitor?"

"I think so," Riceman said unreassuringly. "At least for a while." As he talked, he continued to feed ETHEL instructions and passwords. When the last password took, he sat down.

"Well?" Michelle asked.

"I have to connect the cable."

"Let's do it."

"In a minute. We only have one shot at this thing. If BRUCE discovers she's in his packs, he'll try to kill her—power surge back through the cable."

"How long will we have access?"

"I don't know," Riceman confessed. "I've never done this before. If we're lucky, milliseconds. Maybe only a few nanoseconds. That's long enough for one question."

"What should we ask?"

"I don't know, there's so many. How can we stop the bomb? Why did Saxon activate MERLYN? What is Project Gemini? If the bomb can't be stopped, how can we get the hell out of this dump? Is there a way out? What happened to the people on Levels Two and Three and Four? How do we kill that thing out there?" Riceman could have gone on for hours listing questions. Each one giving birth to a hundred others. But he stopped.

"Choose," he said, as if asking Michelle to choose between two good movies.

She answered instantly with a splutter of choices, "The bomb—how do we get out—Project Gemini—Saxon and MERLYN—the thing."

"And the people?" Riceman asked.

"If the bomb can be stopped, we'll find out later. If it can't, we don't have time to save anyone—maybe not even ourselves. If we can save ourselves, we can use the stuff about Saxon and the project to make sure this never happens again." She paused, then added, "The part about the people—that's rationalization. The truth is—I don't want to know what happened to them."

Riceman didn't press; he knew what she meant. Everyone has a breaking point. This wasn't the time to test hers. He hurriedly keyed in the questions in order of priority, instructed ETHEL where she was to get the information, and tapped the "Enter" key.

ETHEL flashed her response:

QUESTIONS LOGGED. PLEASE CONNECT CABLE.

Riceman quickly connected the cable, returned to the console, and typed:

CABLE CONNE

"Wait," Michelle said. "Better redirect the answers to the printer. If ETHEL goes down, we'll at least have a hard copy."

Riceman erased the cable instruction, typed in the redirection instruction, and retyped:

CABLE CONNECTED

He paused, looked at Michelle, punched the "enter" key.

Almost before his finger was off the key, a large blue snake arced across two of the discpacks, and the Central Processing Unit sounded like a popcorn machine.

"He's got her," Riceman yelled as he headed for the cable. He grabbed the cable, but it had been locked in place by some internal mechanism. He ran back to the keyboard, but it was useless. "He won't turn her loose!"

Michelle wasn't listening. When things had started happening, she had begun a frantic search for something to cut the cable. She had found a paper cutter on a corner desk and was in the process of placing it around the cable. As she forced the slicer down into the cable, a white shock knocked her across the room in a fast tumble that ended against the printer. Paper spewed out of the printer, spilled from the stacker onto her body, and slithered across the floor.

A thick acrid smoke belched from ETHEL's vents, followed by the green, oozing foam of auto-extinguishers. Riceman choked his way towards Michelle as the exhaust fans tried to clear the room.

By the time he got to her, she was already fighting her way out of the paper jungle.

"Are you OK?" he asked.

"Hell no!" she answered, pushing off the last of the paper from her legs. "Did we get anything?"

Riceman looked at the printout. The paper had fed through the printer at such a high speed the print was mostly unreadable. The words of the messages were spread across several pages. After careful study, he was only able to come up with a few complete sentences.

"The first several lines are good. After that it's mostly garbage," he began. "The bomb can be deactivated, but not if the terminals are shut down."

"And Saxon shut them down. What else?"

Riceman ran the printout through his hands till he reached a predetermined spot. "I can't make out too much about Project Gemini—except something went wrong—and it was canceled—secured and canceled."

"The whole project is 'secured and canceled,'" Michelle answered wryly. When it dawned on her what she had said, her face twisted up to Riceman. "Jesus! They've canceled the whole project!"

"Who?"

"Our own government," Michelle shouted till she shook. "They canceled us!"

"Wait a minute," Riceman pleaded, "that's crazy. If they had wanted to do that, they could've just dropped a bomb on us."

"No they couldn't. It had to look like an accident. How could they explain bombing their own people? And besides, the only bomb that could reach us from outside would be a nustome bomb, and they couldn't do that because of the conventional warfare treaty, not even a test. Don't you see?" Michelle was up, pulling his shirt collar. "There's only one bomb that can kill us all, destroy every piece of evidence, every trace of us ever having been here, and we're sitting on it!"

"I don't believe it," Riceman protested with a wave of his hand. "Why would they do that, kill us. I mean—it doesn't make sense!"

"God!" Michelle slapped her forehead with her palm. "Give me strength." She shook her head, turned completely around, and said, "They're crazy. You said it yourself. They're killing a hundred· thousand men and women a month on the two fronts. They wouldn't think twice about blowing us away—for any reason. It could be anything. Maybe they—that's it. They got scared of something. Those cylinders—something—and they pulled the switch. I don't know. But I do know it wasn't a damn accident that triggered ZOMBIE. No one would take a chance of a project this size blowing up—"

"Melting," Riceman interrupted.

"Melting by accident. They did it on purpose!"

"What else?" he prompted.

"I don't know. You think of 'what else.' "

Riceman thought. "Saxon wouldn't let the bomb go off if he didn't have a way out or wasn't already out." It was one of those rare thoughts that actually sounded better when spoken. He took another shot. "That's it. There's got to be a way out of here."

Michelle dropped to her knees and began searching through the printout.

"Up here!" Riceman followed the paper trail across the room, running the printout through his hands as if measuring off yardage. Then he ripped out a section.

"Section 3C." His words didn't sound as impressive as the message had looked on paper.

Michelle looked at the paper. "Doesn't say anything about an exit."

Riceman looked at the message again. "What else could it be? We asked for a way out and this is the only location ETHEL printed."

"That's the only one we can read. Maybe it's not an exit at all."

"Do you have a better idea?"

Michelle looked at the wrinkled paper again. "No."

"Then let's go."

"What about that Gemini thing?" she asked, a little terror cracking into her voice.

"It hasn't bothered us since we've been on this floor," Riceman noted. "Maybe it's dead. Maybe Roselli . . ."

"Sure." Michelle smiled weakly. "Roselli probably killed it."

They looked at each other, both knowing Roselli was dead or lost in the maze of ducting—and there was nothing they could do about it.

Riceman picked up the fire extinguisher and tested it the way Roselli tested the flamethrower. The results were completely different. Instead of a scorching flame, Riceman's finger created a white puff of subzero chemicals. He could hear his father's cynical voice shouting its favorite and universal warning: "You don't stand a snowball's chance in hell, boy!" Now Riceman *was* in hell and holding a snowball machine—and he wondered about the *chance*.

"Better turn off the lights," he said. "Should let our eyes adjust before going."

Michelle stared at him briefly before flipping the light switch, plunging them back into that colorless world where only voices existed.

Riceman could sense what she was thinking, understood why she was staring. It could be the last time they would see each other in full light.

Silence fell between them, each watching the flashlight's ball of light holding steady on the door. Riceman finally reached out and turned the knob.

TIME	:	0517
AREA	:	UNAVAILABLE
LEVEL	:	4
SENSORS	:	1114–15

RICEMAN STEPPED FROM THE ROOM INTO AN AMBER FLOOD of light. The emergency lights, one at each end of the hall and one in the middle, had turned on. He turned his flashlight off and beckoned to Michelle.

"Emergency lights," Riceman commented.

"Why didn't they turn on before, when the lights went out?"

"Nothing works the way it should on this project. Let's hope they stay on."

Michelle was following close on his heels—so close he could feel her breath.

"How far to Section 3—"

"C," Riceman filled in. "I don't know where that is."

She let him get a step ahead of her, then pressed to catch up. "You don't know where we are going?"

"I didn't say that. I know exactly where we are going," he answered slowly. He knew he was talking too much, taking too long to tell her he was heading back to the Security room; but the noise of his voice made everything seem normal; he was as afraid of silence as he was of that Gemini thing—wherever the hell it was hiding.

"Where *are* we going?"

Michelle's words puffed against his neck, warm and gentle as a summer wind. He stopped. Turned to her.

She was a negative. A goddamn negative. Not like black-

'n-white negative. More like one for color prints. The kind he held up to light when he was a kid and wondered where all the color came from. It was magic—now Michelle was magic. He reached out a negative hand and touched her negative face.

"You've never seen this before?" she asked.

"No—you?"

"Once," she answered. "Before I came here. In LA. It's kind of weird."

Scary, Riceman wanted to add. But everything was *scary*. Even Michelle had turned *scary*.

"We're going to Security," he said, still looking at her backwards eyes. "There's a map that'll show us—"

"Where Section 3C is located," she ended.

"Sure," he agreed. He was looking at her, but she wasn't there. Not really. Not like before—in the cream color of the flashlight or the electric blue of the fluorobulbs or even the ink-filled air of the ducts. He was amazed.

He felt her white hair—touched again once fair skin turned grayish red. Without thinking what he was actually doing, he slowly unzipped her jump suit and gazed at the greenish aureoles of her taut breasts.

"Can I help you?" she asked as if she were a salesgirl at Bullocks.

Riceman didn't respond, but he did zip her jump suit back up, slowly. He was several yards farther down the hall before he realized what he had done. He could hear Michelle's steps behind him, not as close as before the exploration, but well within his safety zone. He started to apologize, then decided she probably didn't really notice what happened. Besides, they were at Security and the main subject would be *maps*.

"Hold the door open," he instructed Michelle as he disappeared into the now partially lit room. He tore a large framed map off the wall and set it down in the hall. "I don't see a 3C."

"Here," Michelle pointed.

Riceman twisted his neck in her direction and found himself inches from her chest.

"Down here," she said.

His face flushed light green. He looked at the map—her finger—and a large SECTION 3C.

"No wonder I didn't know where that was. It used to be a large storage room—431 something. They've just changed the name."

"Is there an exit there?" Michelle asked anxiously.

Riceman stood up straight, wiped a nonexistent hair from his forehead, and answered slowly. "Not that I remember." Then added quickly, "Maybe it's hidden. Something like that has got to be hidden. Don't you think?"

Michelle looked at her watch. Five twenty-one. Twenty-two minutes till blast-off—and no straws in sight. "We'll find it—it's there."

In that fleeting bit of silence Riceman took before replying, a muted sound slithered its way towards them like some poisonous snake. Not a menacing sound. Not like the hiss or growl or scratching of something deadly. Just a muted, foreign sound. A sound not of their making, and it scared the hell out of them.

"Did you hear that?" Michelle asked in a suddenly soft, cautious voice.

"It's nothing, maybe a rat," Riceman assured her with false confidence. He managed a forced smile, not much of a weapon against the relentless sound growing louder at the far end of the hall. He stood up from the map, backing slowly away from the noise, his knuckles white from the grip on the fire extinguisher.

They were talking in low, concealed voices, trying to fool themselves and each other into believing they could hide in plain sight. Unlike a rat, the noise did not hesitate in its awkward progress. It knew exactly where they were.

Riceman backed past Michelle. She had frozen like a fawn in the wilderness—natural—instinctive—futile. He grabbed her arm and pulled her after him. Words of caution stuck in his throat, but she understood his gesture and was soon running at his side through the maze of amber halls, past the ones still in the grip of darkness, stopping only briefly to listen for a sound that was sometimes there—sometimes not—sometimes gaining . . .

It was while passing one of the darkened corridors in a

dead run that Riceman caught the glint of something metallic. He stopped without warning. Michelle almost crashed into him, missing by inches.

"What's wrong?" she asked, breathless, fear pulling her onward.

"Maybe nothing," he answered softly. "Wait here."

But she did not, following him into the side corridor—into the inky darkness that suffocated her, to that bent object halfway down. Riceman flicked on his flashlight. The ball of light worked slowly over the flamethrower. He handed the extinguisher and flashlight to Michelle, picked up the flamethrower's nozzle, and tested it. Empty. Michelle played the light along a broken, splotchy trail of blood, disappearing under a nearby door.

Her voice shrill now, fighting the panic. "Let's go now. I want to go!"

Riceman wanted to go too. Wanted to run—to never look back—but could not. He took the flashlight from Michelle's trembling hand and moved slowly towards the door. He fought back the haunting images of his youth—of things dark and hideous leaping from closets in the night. Riceman forced his hand to the doorknob, turned slightly, and pushed.

Michelle slunk back into the darkness of the hall; she did not want to see, but she knew Riceman must. He entered the room and closed the door behind him.

His light slid across the bodies of eighty or ninety men. Some lying where they had been thrown, most of them stacked along one wall like cords of wood. The stench filled his lungs. As he looked at them, his back stiffened with horror as some of them looked back—their heads rolling uncontrollably, and their eyes a sightless picture of the torture they had endured.

"Help me." The voice was Roselli's, but Riceman stood paralyzed as the light fell on the barely recognizable face. "Help me—please."

"Roselli?" Riceman asked, afraid of the answer.

"Yes."

"You'll be all right," Riceman promised, rushing to him and kneeling beside the living corpse.

"No—my knife . . ."

Roselli's gun was missing, but the knife was still tied to his side. Riceman pulled it out, the handle almost too big for his hand.

"I have it," he told Roselli.

"Kill me."

"What?"

"All the bones below my neck have been dissolved, but it won't let any of us die—until—we—are needed," Roselli choked out, his face grimacing with pain.

The next question caught in Riceman's throat. "Why does it need you?"

The pain grew. Tears streamed down Roselli's face. He had hoped Riceman would have guessed, because he didn't want to say it. "It wants us fresh."

The whisper rang in Riceman's ears. He felt the room spin as his light flew around it and stopped on a table. On it was the half-eaten corpse of an old man. The vomit came and there was no holding it back, until Riceman emptied his soul on the floor.

The bomb would soon end Roselli's pain, but even a minute would seem an eternity to him. Just before Riceman thrust the knife, he took a final look at Roselli and whispered, "You got him, got him good."

Roselli smiled for the last time; then it was over.

Riceman was tired. He wanted to let everything slip peacefully out of his memory. He wanted to sleep, to melt with all of the things he had grown to hate. For an instant, less than the blink of an eye, he relaxed. Then Michelle's scream sent him headlong into the amber world.

She was backing away haltingly, her head tilted like a wild thing smelling fire. Her body was shaking in revulsion as she stared back over Riceman's shoulder.

Riceman whirled, knife in hand. His knees went numb. The knot in his stomach spread throughout his body. He held the scream in his throat until it came out as an unrecognizable noise, as unrecognizable as the thing coming towards him.

It was still half a hallway from him, but even at that

distance Riceman could see more than he wanted to—more than he could force his eyes from.

It walked as if it were wounded or hurt, but that wasn't the first thing Riceman noticed. First he saw the maddened eyes—red and piercing from so far away. Slanted, almost human, the eyes of death. It stood at the far end of the hall, in an amber lit corridor, its eyes burning through the dark air to Riceman, burning through him . . . holding him; its cruel mouth moved mechanically, its lips pulled high over gleaming fangs.

While Riceman's body was partially paralyzed, his mind was not. Every feature of the thing was fed into that part that sorted facts and figures without emotion—facts he needed for survival.

Thing—Gemini—wounded—fangs—stay away from them—height—seven feet—no skin—all muscles and sinew exposed—color unknown—damn the light.

All stored. Digested in that instant between when Riceman first saw the creature and when it started moving toward him.

"Go—go!" Riceman could hear himself shrill with fear that Michelle was frozen, unable to run—to get away. The creature might get past him to her and . . .

He grabbed her roughly by the upper arm and pulled her unwilling body down the hall. With every step, her legs seemed to work a little better.

"Don't look back," he ordered, running in back now, pushing. He tried not to look back himself, but he knew he had to, if even for an instant, to see if it was gaining. Then suddenly he didn't have to look back. He felt its decaying breath close to him—to her.

Michelle's muscles were still stricken by Its' face. Each time he shoved her with less effort, but recovery was not fast enough. Though some unseen injury had slowed the creature to a wounded pace, it would be on them before Michelle fully recovered.

Riceman snatched the fire extinguisher from her limp grasp, pushed one last time, and whirled on the pressing thing.

It was closer than he had hoped. He had planned to

point the extinguisher at it. Bluff long enough for Michelle to recover. Long enough for her to call to him and run with him, but there was no time. By the time he pulled the trigger, releasing a cold foam of fluff, the thing was almost on him.

The low hiss of the extinguisher was mixed with the chilling cry of the creature as it fell back. It cringed defensively, sheltering itself with a grotesque arm until it found safety by plunging down a side hall.

The unparalyzed had become paralyzed.

Riceman stood dumbfounded and confused.

His sudden and unexpected victory had left him completely without a plan of action. Things had definitely not worked out to his expectations. He had been fully aware he was going to die. Even had counted on it to a large degree.

In that blink of eternity between pulling the trigger and seeing the spewing flakes, he had decided he was going to die a horrible death, and had thus disconnected himself from his soon-to-be-damaged body. But nothing worked out right. The creature had whined off faster than it had chased him, leaving Riceman's body trying to convince his brain that he was still alive.

"Come on!"

This time it was Michelle pleading, pulling, red with fear. And this time it was Riceman who stumbled down the hall trying to decide what had gone wrong.

By the time his brain had taken up residence, they were hopelessly lost in a maze of unmarked crisscrossing corridors.

"Where are we?" they asked each other in unison.

"Don't you know?"

"I wasn't watching where we were going," Riceman admitted as Michelle used the flashlight to search for room numbers on the many doors. "You won't find any. That's because of security. You had to know where you were going to get there. Kept people from wandering around and poking into things they shouldn't."

"That's stupid! How could anyone find anything?"

"By the room number," he explained, "1204R03L08DR means twelve corridors straight from the elevator, then four to the right, three left, then the eighth door on the right. Simple."

"Stupid!"

"Simply stupid." Riceman half smiled. "We have to get back to Security, to the elevator, and start from there. It's the only way."

"And how do we do that?"

"Luck," Riceman wanted to say, but luck was what got them into the mess and he doubted it would get them out.

"Luck," he said anyway. It came out even more hollow sounding than he had thought. "Maybe we should spread out."

"No."

"We could cover more corridors that way," he suggested.

"No!"

"Not far. Within shouting distance."

"No!"

They began their search together, Michelle refusing to stray more than three feet from his side; Riceman still wondering why the creature had been frightened by a puff of harmless white smoke; both of them listening for a foreign sound in their amber world that had suddenly grown silent.

The corridors were not straight. The amber-lit ones ran in concentric circles, the black ones radiating out from the center like spokes of a wheel. Michelle wanted to stay in the light, but Riceman decided to stick to the dark. He reasoned that since Security was located on an amber corridor, he would be able to cover more by using the black spokes to cross them, or something like that. He had it clear in his mind, but he was really operating on a feeling; it was something that he couldn't explain, but it was there—pressing him, telling him he was right.

One thing was working for them, the creature had disappeared. They stopped several times to listen for its sound—nothing. Strange, Riceman thought. But he didn't want to tempt fate by questioning it. Fate had a way of answering that scared the hell out of him. He stopped to examine his torn ankle. Not that it bothered him. In fact, he had forgotten about it, but Michelle asked about it and he felt he had to show her it was better, even though he didn't want to look at the jagged crimson rip, pierced by the sickly white of a bone.

"Feels much better," he said, holding his foot, ankle bared, up to the scrutiny of the flashlight and Michelle's examination.

"Looks better," she said with an almost startled tone. She looked closer, then nodded, reaffirming her diagnosis. "Better."

Riceman looked. It was better, or maybe he had just thought it was worse than it was. He could have sworn the bone had been showing.

When they found Security and the map, their joy was short. Michelle looked at her watch and announced the bomb would detonate in eight minutes, thirteen seconds. Riceman tore off that section of the map with the room code for Section 3C and they were soon running and counting and forgetting that something else was down there with them.

"Here," Riceman shouted, pointing to a door.

They each looked at the code again. 1411R07L11DR. Eleventh door on the right. They counted, moved down one door, and pushed it open without noticing it had already been broken open. They stepped tentatively into the dimly lit room.

What light there was radiated outward from the center of the room, casting long shadows across the banks of test equipment and monitors that lined the walls. The source of the light was a glass tank of luminescent liquid bubbling between two horizontal cylinders. The menacing hiss of escaping gas pounded in their ears.

Riceman's grip tightened on the extinguisher as he stepped forward cautiously, Michelle at his back sweeping the walls with the flashlight, one hand clutching his arm.

The cylinders were exactly as Saxon had described them, except now their coffinlike lids were open. Riceman took the flashlight, but Michelle refused to take her eyes off the dancing shadows playing on the walls.

The insides of the cylinders were lined with a thick, hard white substance that brought to mind the picture of Hank's severed finger lying on the dirt. The memory of the flesh eaten from the bleached bones pushed Riceman back against Michelle.

"What's wrong?" she asked.

Something, he thought without answering, but he couldn't quite grasp it. Bone—crushed ground—reformed as a lining. Why? The cylinders were obviously designed to keep something inside—something that wanted out. A new fear swept across Riceman.

"There!" Michelle shouted, pointing across the room.

Riceman flashed the light—nothing.

"There was something!" she insisted.

He didn't look again. If there had been something hiding, he hoped it would stay hidden until they left. He sure as hell wasn't about to flush it out.

Michelle tightened her grip on his arm. "Let's find 3C and get out of here!" she pleaded.

Riceman knew she was right. Forget about the cylinders. Forget about the human-bone lining. Forget the probing questions and get the hell out!

The bubbling liquid was connected to the cylinders by long tubes of clear plastic. Riceman touched the tubes, then the surface of a cylinder. Subzero. The liquid was a cooling agent that ran between the metallic skin and the bone lining. A return tube ran from underneath the cylinders back to the glass tank.

"It's the cold," Riceman whispered as if saying it too loudly would make it not so.

"What?"

"Remember that guy in the freezer?" Riceman asked, but didn't wait for an answer. "He was safe in there because the creature couldn't stand the cold." He was excited now, waving his hands with meaningless gestures, the flashlight beam cutting through the air. "And it ran from the extinguisher because the carboiden flakes are freezing. Don't you see? And," he looked back at the cylinders, almost afraid to say what he thought, "the cylinders aren't from a crashed UFO. They're from Earth—Saxon lied about them."

"Why?"

"I don't know. Maybe Mother lied to him. Maybe he really thought they were from outer space."

"Why would Mother lie?"

Before he could tell her he didn't know that either, the sound of something heavy crashed towards them through the darkness.

Michelle fell back. Riceman pulled the extinguisher's trigger an instant before he brought the flashlight to rest on the cringing creature as it stumbled screeching behind the protection of some large cabinets. Adrenaline kept his finger pressed too long, and the belching cloud faded to a whisper.

Riceman could hear the creature clamoring behind the cabinets for shelter, but knew it would be back. Michelle tugged on his arm, pulling him back—back towards the hissing sound he had heard when he first entered the room.

Riceman pointed the flashlight towards the hiss. It was coming from a tank of liquid nitrogen used to cool the bubbling liquid. He handed the flashlight to Michelle, instructed her to hold it on the tank, turned the knob at the top of the tank until the hiss stopped, and started to disconnect the tube with a wrench that hung from the tank by a wire.

A sound from the far side of the room pulled the light to it.

"Never mind that!" Riceman shouted until Michelle shined the shaking light back on the tank and his fumbling wrench.

The sound grew louder, working its way toward them, but Michelle held the light as steady as fear would let her. The wrench kept slipping—caught—slipped again—each slip stopping Michelle's heart. As the thrashing, angry sound got closer to her back, she moved closer to the tank, to Riceman.

The table she had just been leaning on crashed across the room as the wrench turned the nut one last time. As the tube fell from the tank, Michelle fell forward, twisting as she fell until the flashlight beam fell full across the blistered head of the creature.

Riceman gave the knob a turn, sending frozen death toward the creature in a billowing cloud. He followed the screaming thing across the room to a corner, where he trapped it until it was dead. He didn't realize Michelle had followed him until he heard the small stifled cry in her throat. The flashlight was still shaking, but she held it on the creature even now.

The electric buzz of her wristwatch alarm upstaged their moment of victory.

"Five minutes," Michelle announced as she stopped the impersonal warning.

A brief search found the opening to Section 3C behind a cabinet. It was an exhaust duct large enough for the creature. The coincidence of a duct large enough for the creature to use, on the same level where the creature was kept, stuck with Riceman as he crawled after Michelle. Another question nagged at his mind. If there was a way out, why didn't the creature use it? It didn't know about the bomb, but it did know Riceman was down there and had the ability to kill it. So why didn't it escape? It was either stupid, or afraid.

A sizzling, popping sound echoed through the duct after them.

"It's started," Michelle shouted back as they broke out of the duct into the exhaust shaft.

There was no fan. That fact only whizzed through Riceman's mind, not stopping long enough to plant a question, chased out by the sounds of destruction whistling from the duct. Firmly attached to the far side of the shaft was a ladder stretching upwards into the black hole.

That's when Riceman's mind finally connected the size of the duct and the mysterious ladder. They were part of a plan—an escape plan for the creatures—the Gemini. Mother *wanted* the things to escape.

It was then he realized the holes in the Level Two exhaust fan and duct cover were not made by something trying to get out, but rather in.

Riceman felt the answers to all his questions were waiting for him at the top of the ladder.

"We'll never make it," Michelle said.

Riceman didn't argue; he knew she was right. It was too far and they were out of time. His flashlight caught the glint of a rail running beside the ladder and quickly followed it down to a maintenance hoist.

"We'll take the 'A' train," he explained, snapping her buckle to his belt, then snapping himself to the hoist.

He didn't know a damn thing about hoists, but he had seen kids jumpstart cars. He bridged the gap between two contacts with a buckle . . . nothing.

"Stop fucking around!" Michelle yelled.

With that and the acid bomb as incentives, he tried again . . . buzz . . . flash . . . up.

Several times during the ascent, Riceman lost contact . . . the hoist stopped . . . Michelle cussed . . . Riceman got the motor going again.

A hundred feet from the top, a bright blue arc jolted them to a dead stop. The hoist slipped three feet . . . caught itself, slipped again. On the last stop, Riceman swung to the ladder, detached himself from the hoist, and pulled Michelle clear as it plummeted out of sight.

When she steadied herself on the ladder, Riceman unsnapped her from his belt and pulled her up past him . . . then pushed her onward.

Michelle started the slow unsteady climb. Each rung was to be her last, but then she forced another and another, until her hands reached the top. One more pull and she lay gasping for fresh air under the star-laced sky.

Riceman pulled himself into the night air, and lay on the damp ground beside her. He had gotten his second wind. Or was it his fifth? He remembered feeling exhausted, then a new strength infused him. He stood looking at the shaft's cover—heavy carbolium steel. The anchor brackets had been eaten through and the entire cover dislocated from its intended position by several feet as if made from Styrofoam.

Three hundred yards beyond the cover, the main compound of Project Gemini lay burning. Even from that distance, Riceman could feel the scorching heat. Back over his shoulder, approximately four hundred yards away, was the surplus yard with its ammunition bunker, barrels of fuel oil, and lumber. Burning debris was scattered over the entire compound, even reaching the seven hundred yards from the Belium tower to the surplus area.

There was a rumble under their feet, and a hiss from deep in the shaft. Riceman grabbed Michelle, pulled her to her feet, and pushed her towards safety . . . away from the acrid smell of burnt flesh. He wondered about the people trapped in the structure, had Saxon ever told them what to expect? Halfway to the surplus area, there was a thunderous roar as acid shot from the exhaust shaft like a Texas gusher. The death rain splattered behind them, making retreat impossible. Running now, eyes searching for shelter, Riceman steered Michelle towards the ammunition bunker. Less than a hundred yards. Then seventy . . . the gusher subsided and a dark figure stepped into view from behind the bunker.

He was larger than he remembered. Grotesque . . . mishapen . . . and lit only by the flicker of burning debris; Riceman knew it was Saxon. Michelle dropped to her knees and gave Riceman a warning tug, but he pulled away from her, ventured a little closer, then stopped. Saxon was dragging the limp form of a creature like the one Riceman had killed. Sporadically, without cause or warning, he would raise the thing up like a child enraged at a rag doll, and slam it down with a sickening thud that echoed clearly through the night air.

The dead thing was of monstrous proportions, but Saxon flung it through the air effortlessly. If there was going to be a fight, Riceman had no doubt about the outcome. As he watched Saxon drag his ragged toy to the top of a small knoll in front of the ammunition bunker, he reached his hand into his pocket and felt the pitifully frail weapon; the small pocket knife Michelle found on Level 4.

Saxon looked up, his voice rasping over hardened vocal cords. "Did you kill yours?"

Comrades. Teammates. Allies. Riceman rejected the thought and answered with as little emotion as the question had asked for.

"Yes."

"And," Saxon said, sitting down, the dead thing's neck squeezed under his arm, its face looking up at him in awe. "You have questions?"

Saxon's new position was less menacing to Riceman, allowing him to cautiously close the gap between them to less than thirty yards.

"A few," Riceman answered, wondering why Saxon didn't just come down and kill him if that was what he meant to do. "But there's not much use. You'll just lie." The knowledge that he was going to die gave him a new freedom. It didn't matter what he said, things couldn't get worse.

Saxon shifted his position slightly, then answered without emotion. "I won't have to lie to you now."

Riceman walked a few steps closer. He could see clearly the blistered dark skin covering Saxon's face, neck, and arm. His artificial arm gleamed in the night, catching the flickering flames that surrounded him and sending long spears of orange flashing down at Riceman.

"What's happened to you?"

"Belium," Saxon answered softly, almost reverently.

"The stuff your arm is made of?"

"Yes."

"I don't understand."

"You will."

Riceman was less than twenty yards from Saxon. Close enough to whisper, though he didn't mean to . . .

"You're dying . . ."

Saxon laughed even harder, temporarily dropping his dead toy, then snatching it back up with renewed vengeance, and at last looking at Riceman with piercing eyes.

"You're a fool!"

"No. I used to be a fool, but I gave it up."

"Well then ex-fool, you better get on with your questions!"

"What about Rita?" Riceman shouted. "You said you knew who killed her and you'd get him." It was an insignificant detail, one death among the hundreds, but Riceman wanted to challenge Saxon with what now seemed a minor happening.

"That's right," Saxon admitted. "I do know who killed her, and you could say I got him in a way."

"Roselli?"

"Me." The answer came as the punch line to a wonderful joke, with a laugh that rolled down from the knoll.

The laughter dredged Rita's gaping red smile up from that dark corner of Riceman's mind where it had been hiding.

"For God's sake, why?"

"Why did I slit her throat? Or why did I stuff her in your closet?"

"Both!"

"She knew too much about me. She tried to tell Roselli, but he didn't believe her. There was no other way. Really a shame; she could have had everything."

"Why my closet? And why make it look like Roselli did it?"

"I knew Mother had activated ZOMBIE and I needed to send you down to the fourth level. I also knew you wouldn't go. So what better way of getting you down there than by sending Miss Montignac on the mission with a killer. Of course you followed . . . to protect her . . . two lambs." Saxon roared with laughter, pleased with a secret yet to be unfolded.

"Bullshit!" Riceman yelled. "You didn't need me on Level Four. There was no way to stop ZOMBIE, and you knew it!"

Saxon poised himself into a crouch and seemed about to rush Riceman, then he lowered himself. Riceman looked to a movement at the back of the bunker. It was Michelle. She had found a large pipe and was edging for position behind Saxon.

"Why me?" Riceman asked again.

Saxon didn't answer. He poked one of the creature's eyes out and popped it into his mouth.

"Cannibals eat their enemies to get their strength. It works!" Saxon said, sucking the squeezed juices back as they slithered from the corners of his mouth. He bit into the second eye.

Riceman could feel the bottom of his stomach coming up through his throat, but he managed to force it back. Michelle had disappeared around behind the bunker and was probably sneaking along one side to get at Saxon's back.

"Why would Mother want to destroy this project—the Gemini?"

"You talking about this?" Saxon held up the eyeless head of the creature. "Don't you know what this is?"

"No, but it didn't come from any fucking UFO!"

"Good boy," Saxon smiled. "This is a Cannese Wambat." Again the laughter, tapering down to a thin rattle . . . "I think it used to be a man like you and me. But the Cannese were losing the war. They needed a weapon. Didn't matter what—a good weapon." Saxon held the creature's jaw open wider than was possible, then wider until the jawbone cracked with a shot. "It was a good one."

"But it couldn't stand cold, the CanAm front."

"Right," Saxon agreed. "But nothing could stop it in Brazil . . . not until now."

"And you stopped it."

"And so did you," Saxon pointed out. He held the creature's head up like a puppet and worked the slack jaw. "So . . . did . . . you." Laughter. . . .

"I heard." Riceman started, slouching his shoulders in a nonmenacing manner, shuffling slowly closer to Saxon, hand in his pocket around the knife. "The Cannese were working with chromosome restructuring. Is that how they did it?"

"Maybe . . . maybe not. I don't know."

"And you?" Riceman asked, moving ever so slowly.

"Belium. Lost my arm in some war. It doesn't matter. They wanted to kick me out!" Saxon's eyes flashed up. "Said I was 'disabled.' Like that. Fuck me! Just like that . . . wasn't right!"

"But they gave you this opportunity instead."

"They don't 'give' anything—unless they 'want' something."

"Mother spent a lot of money on this project." He was less than ten yards from Saxon. There was a way to kill him . . . maybe. "Why would She want to destroy it?"

"Why do you think?" Saxon smiled, the partial remains of an eye slithered between his teeth and gums.

"Mother wanted to test you against them." Riceman pointed at the dead creature. Nine yards.

"She was afraid of me," Saxon replied with a strange lack of emotion. "You see, during the operation for the arm, they put a monitor inside my head."

"To monitor your brainwaves?" Eight yards. Riceman could see the edge of Michelle's face at the corner of the bunker.

"What they saw scared them; they wanted out. Abort! Abort! All their fucking little hearts going thump, thump, thump. They were scared." Then Saxon added, "They had a right to be."

"So the bomb was meant to kill you." Riceman inched. "But Mother still wanted the test. So She unleashed the Gemini." Six yards. He saw Michelle looking . . . shook his head. Not yet.

"Haven't you guessed by now?" Saxon asked.

"What?"

"The secret," Saxon rasped with glee. "I lied to you about the good secret."

"What lie?" Four yards. Nerves humming.

"When I told you the project was named after those two cylinders. But you don't understand . . . you'll never understand. You were a mistake."

"You think so?" Riceman wasn't listening closely, he was within three yards . . . nine feet.

"And now you are trying to kill me with that stupid little knife in your pocket, hoping Michelle will distract me while you plunge the little dagger into my heart. Stupid little man. So sad now. Experiment gone bad. Abort! Abort!" Saxon cast the dead carcass aside and stood up. "Too bad. Nothing could have stopped us. We could have ruled the world!" He picked up a steel bar as Michelle emerged from her hiding place. *"Look at me,"* he ordered her. *"I am Gemini!"*

Lunging from the knoll, Saxon swung at Riceman. He missed, but Riceman didn't have a chance to counter. Michelle circled behind Saxon, waiting for a chance to hit with her rod and run. Riceman tightened his grip on the knife; he had to get in close, so close he would be able to smell the slime that covered Saxon's hands. Riceman and Michelle circled Saxon like wolves on a winter kill.

Riceman began to work backwards towards the bunker. It wasn't logical or planned; he was working by instinct. Michelle closed the gap to Saxon's back, but he didn't even look around. He swung again; this time Riceman felt the wind from the tip of the rod as it skirted past him and cut through the bunker wall like a scalpel through flesh.

Saxon, enraged by the wall, battered away at it until there was a gaping hole in the side of the bunker. Michelle rushed Saxon and bashed his head with the rod. Saxon whirled without a flinch, caught her by the throat, and threw her against the wall. He swung back with his hand, hitting Riceman below the right shoulder in mid-lunge, and sending him sprawling across the tops of the oil barrels.

Riceman lay recovering from the near fatal blow as Saxon turned back to Michelle. Pinning her against the wall like a beautiful butterfly, Saxon stripped off her clothing with one swift move. She drove her foot into his groin repeatedly, and still he smiled at her.

"Kill me you sonofabitch, or I'll kill you!" she yelled, her breasts heaving violently in the flickering light from nearby fires.

"Rita turned me down," Saxon said. "Don't make that mistake! A God needs sons." His hand found her breast and squeezed till she cried out. She struggled, but it was of little use. He took her on the ground, in the same manner any wild animal mates. When it was over, he held his hand to her throat until she passed out.

Riceman was dazed, but he still had the knife. He could see Saxon coming to finish the job. Riceman laid very still. As Saxon swung down with the steel rod, he rolled. The rod sunk into the barrel, splattering them with thick, slippery oil. Saxon swung again, and a second barrel was split. Riceman kept a tight grip on the knife, knowing that if any oil got under his fingers, he would lose it. Oil covered the ground under Saxon's feet, and on the next swing, he slipped and fell on Riceman.

There was an instant when Saxon was disoriented. It was then that Riceman drove the knife to its hilt into the only vital part of Saxon: his eye. Riceman heard a squishing as the blade sliced through its mark, and felt the tip sink deep into Saxon's brain.

Saxon roared with pain. He tried to rip the knife out, but the oil on his hands stopped him. He bent backwards in agony. Riceman kicked out with both feet, hit Saxon square on the chest, and knocked him back toward the ammunition bunker.

As Saxon grappled with the knife, Riceman leaped from the barrels, raced to Michelle, and effortlessly scooped her up with one arm. As he carried her off, he looked back at Saxon struggling with the knife, and realized it was not a fatal blow. Riceman picked up a heavy stick, rubbed the end of his clothes until it was covered with oil, and stuck it into some burning debris. Once aflame, he threw it at Saxon.

Saxon ignited instantly, becoming a human torch. Riceman carried Michelle to the fringe of the compound and laid her down behind a large knoll. He looked toward the bunker in time to see Saxon standing like a great broken cross, burning in the night. Saxon roared one final defiant cry, then tumbled backwards into the bunker. The explosion lit up the sky, but Riceman could not bear to watch. The explosion of Saxon, combined with the maddening sound of rushing acid as it melted the underground structure, was overwhelming. Riceman covered Michelle with his body, shielding her from falling debris, and waited for the insanity to end.

When it was over, he gathered Michelle in his arms, carried her to the far edge of the compound, leaned back against a fallen lamp post and waited for the shadowed blue edging along the mountain ridges to change to the golden light of morning.

Still deep in the half-light of the valley, Riceman held Michelle close and thought about the surface world gone mad. Starvation—wars—riots. Maybe Saxon wasn't so wrong about conquering the world. At least there would be one leader. How bad could life be without the constant threat of death? No more secret projects. No more war. There would be something to live for. There would be peace then. It would not be an easy thing to do. Many people would die in the beginning . . .

A movement from Michelle pushed the wild thoughts from Riceman's mind. He started to stroke her hair, but he changed his mind when he saw his oil covered hand. It was then he noticed his last connection with Project Gemini. A memento. A small token given him in a private ceremony by Saxon. It was meant as a joke, but Riceman had worn it with pride. In the blue light of the early morning, he pulled the ring off, felt its softness and warmth one last time, and tossed it toward the center of the compound.

If there had been more light, Riceman would have noticed the stark difference between the black oil on his hand and the dark gray band of metallic skin around his finger . . . it was spreading. . . .

EPILOGUE

THE AREA IN AND AROUND THE AMMUNITION BUNKER WAS excavated to a depth of six feet. No trace of Colonel C. P. Saxon was ever found.

The official records of Project Gemini show no survivors.